# THE
# IMMORTAL

An Edward Mendez, P. I. Thriller

Book 3

Gerard Denza

The Immortal:
An Edward Mendez, P. I. Thriller
Book III

This novel is entirely a work of fiction. The names, characters, and incidents portrayed in it are the work of the author's imagination. Any resemblance to actual persons, living or dead, events or locations, is entirely incidental.

Cover art: Book Covers Art

www.gerarddenza.com

Also available digitally.

# BY THE SAME AUTHOR:

ICARUS: THE COLLECTED PLAYS

RAMSAY: DEALER OF DEATH

THE TIME DECEIVER:
An Edward Mendez, P. I. Thriller, Book I

NIGHT DRIFTER:
An Edward Mendez, P. I. Thriller, Book II

THE IMMORTAL:
An Edward Mendez, P. I. Thriller, Book III

# Main Characters:

1) **Edward Mendez:** a private investigator who knows that the serial killer in New York City is out to kill him.

2) **Angel Ulysses Correa:** an immortal and a cold-blooded murderer who has come to accept his new life.

3) **Wulf Holderman:** a Nazi who invited the wrong man into his book shop.

4) **Jack Marino:** the new elevator operator in Edward's office building.

5) **Lt. William Donovan:** needs Edward Mendez to help him track down the serial killer who may not be human.

6) **Sgt. Tom Rayno:** an agreeable young man who finds himself teamed up with Edward Mendez.

7) **Dottie Mendez:** Edward's sister who wants her brother to investigate a missing person's case.

8) **Marlena Lake:** a woman who revels in danger. She is visited by a stranger who is an adept liar.

9) **Susan Broder:** Marlena's practical daughter who finds herself mixing drinks for a possible killer.

10) **Turhan Aswan:** a funeral parlor director who heads a contraband ring with a deadly and ancient secret. He is not what he appears to be.

11) **Stripes:** Dottie's tabby cat.

12) **Hector Correa:** the father of an immortal and a serial killer. He can't face the truth about his son.

13) **Louisa Correa:** the mother of an immortal and a serial killer. A woman who won't give into blackmail.

14) **Tess:** Valerie Vandor's landlady who may have uncovered a vital piece of evidence that links her former tenant to the serial killer.

15) **Randy Bates:** a gymnasium worker who knew Angel Correa and didn't like him.

16) **Eva Ceres:** a nursing student and an innocent victim.

17) **Ellen Barnett:** a postal worker who is the last to see Eva Ceres alive.

18) **Yolanda Estravades:** an amateur ice skater and Edward's girlfriend.

19) **Henriette Miller:** a nursing student and a friend of Eva Ceres.

20) **Professor Daniel Gifford:** a teacher at Hunter College who may have seen something that he shouldn't have.

21) **Anna Chan:** a beautiful young woman who has recently become an American citizen. She has given refuge to Angel Correa for a price.

22) **Jaime Morillo:** Angel's workout buddy at the gym who sees a drastic change in his best friend.

23) **Isolde Himmel:** a seemingly sophisticated woman who must ask a favor of Marlena Lake. She knows a great many things.

24) **Henry Vandor:** Valerie's father who refused the gift of immortality.

25) **Valerie Vandor:** a bohemian and a member of Turhan Aswan's group. Angel has vowed to kill her for betraying him.

26) **Consuelo Morillo:** Jaime's sister who is in love with Angel.

27) **Diane Price:** a member of Aswan's group.

28) **Juan Ortega:** a member of Aswan's group.

29) **Aniika Aswan:** Aswan's wife. It is she who runs the "business."

30) **Mohamed:** it is he who shanghais Angel.

31) **Tony Monteo:** the police Medical Officer and a friend of Edward's.

32) **Nella Mendez:** Edward's sister and part-time secretary and accountant.

33) **Nathalie Montaigne:** an ex-patriot of France who runs into a series of coincidences which may prove dangerous for her and her neighbors.

34) **Werner Hoffman:** a close friend of Nathalie's who is still interested in the secret of Edward's mother.

35) **Catrina Mendez:** Edward's sister who is recovering from third degree burns.

36) **Edith Burton:** mother of a young boy, Tommy, who may be the sole witness to a crime committed weeks ago during the sun's disappearance.

37) **Grace Stone:** Edith's sister whose daughter may be a witness to the same crime as Tommy.

38) **Ricky:** a young, black man who is riding in a subway car with a serial killer.

39) **Cora:** Ricky's girlfriend who tries to warn him off danger.

# TABLE OF CONTENTS

# Prologue

THE TWO men walked into the book shop. The sun had just reappeared in the sky and for a few moments, neither man could see in the darkness of the shop. Wulf Holderman was about to turn on the overhead light when Angel Correa stopped him.

-Why did you do that? Don't you want to see?

-My eyes are adjusting. Yours will, too.

The young man looked around the shop.

-You own this book shop?

-Of course. For many years. Why do you ask?

-Just asking. You read all these books?

-Many of them.

Angel took one of the books off the shelf.

-This looks pretty old, but it's in real good condition.

-You interested in the esoteric?

-I don't know what that word means. You mind telling me?

-It means, to put it roughly, the philosophical...things that interest only a few knowledgeable people. The subjects can include philosophy or even the supernatural.

-The supernatural, huh? Funny you should say that.

Angel Correa ran his fingers along one of the bookshelves.

-No dust. You got some woman coming in to do your housework?

-No. I think you wanted to use the bathroom?

-Yeah. Where is it?

-Follow me to the back room. I can see better now.

The two men walked to the back room. Wulf Holderman pointed out the small bathroom to his visitor who walked in. He closed the door behind him.

-Strange young man, but not unattractive.

A few minutes passed by and Wulf Holderman was starting to grow impatient. He wanted to collect his money that he'd hidden and get out of the city as fast as possible. He was a man wanted by the police for further questioning: questions that he might have a hard time answering...questions about his Nazi comrades who'd been responsible for the sun's disappearance.

The bathroom door opened and Angel stepped out. He'd taken off his bomber jacket and his T-shirt. He stood in the open doorway stripped to the waist and staring at Wulf.

-Making yourself comfortable? Don't get too cozy because I have to leave soon.

Angel approached Wulf.

-I felt kind of warm. Thought I might wash up. Do you mind?

-Frankly, yes. I'm in a hurry.

-You ducking the cops or something?

Wulf flinched at the young man's perceptiveness. Angel moved closer...invading Wulf's personal space.

-What we can do can be done real quick. I'm being friendly. Catch my drift?

Wulf understood. And, his erection told Angel that he understood. Angel placed his hand in back of Wulf's head.

-Give us a kiss...just like the ancient Greeks. Just like you want to. It'll mean a lot to me. And, then, I'll leave.

Wulf placed his mouth on Angel's lips...Angel forced his tongue into Wulf's mouth and began to draw the blood from his first victim. Wulf struggled but couldn't free himself. And, then, Angel took out his dagger and plunged it into Wulf's solar plexus. The book shop owner's body went limp. And, in another few moments, he lay rotting on the floor of his book shop.

Angel Correa had baptized himself.

# Part I
# Edward Mendez

# Chapter One
# January 4, 1948
# A.M.

EDWARD MENDEZ pulled on his black polo shirt. At last, he was fully dressed and out of that damned hospital bed. It had been nearly three weeks of seeing a dissipating green mist blocking his vision; but, now it was gone and the P. I.'s eyesight was razor sharp: almost too sharp. He gazed at the fingers of his left hand. He could see the tiny hairs and lines as he'd never before seen them. He looked over at his duffel bag on the floor; man, it looked kind of beat up. He never noticed all the varied discolorations before.

And, then, he gazed out of the hospital window. The sunlight was dazzling and the sky was a brilliant china-blue.

He turned away from the window. The newspaper on the bed caught Edward's eye. He pushed it aside to sit down and put on his shoes. A headline on page three caught his eye: "New York City Has A Serial Killer." He read the article.

"The remains of a fifth murder victim were found the other night in the West Village near to where Martin Ho's body was found. The latest victim has been identified as Adele Locke: a part-time waitress and aspiring young actress who had only recently moved to New York City from St. Louis. The medics haven't been able to fix an exact time or day of the killing. The body was in a state of decay but still recognizable as a corpse...unlike the other murder victims who've been found. Miss Locke's handbag was next to the body and it's believed to be hers. The police are interrogating everyone in the vicinity of the restaurant last night. So far, there are no suspects."

Edward smiled wryly.

-A serial killer at large, huh? Surprised it didn't make the front page. I wonder if Lt. Donovan is in on this case? I'll have to ring him up when I get the chance later.

Edward finished putting on his shoes while mentally making out a schedule of what to do when he checked out of the hospital. It was just 10 o'clock so he decided to head on over to his office in downtown Manhattan to check up on things. He would have stopped off at his girlfriend's place but she would be at the ice rink in midtown practicing for the upcoming figure skating nationals. He didn't want to distract her. She'd been on edge for the past few day and Edward felt she'd be better off focusing on "straight" lines and "figure-eights." He laced up his shoes, put on his leather jacket, gathered up his duffel bag and was about to walk out of his room to go to the nurse's station without his Fedora.

The phone on the night stand rang. Edward picked it up.

-Edward Mendez.

-Good morning, my love. It's Yolanda. Have they served you your breakfast yet?

-Yolanda, baby! Yep. Had breakfast and I'm checking out a day early.

-Today? I would have come down to pick you up. Why didn't you tell me?

-I didn't know until I woke up. You know I'm the impulsive type. Are you at the ice rink?

-Of course. I took a five minute break to call. Are you sure that you're ready to leave?

-If I don't, I'll go stark raving mad. I'm just not the bedridden type. I'll try and drop by the rink later.

-Just leave a message if you call. But, try and come by.

-I will.

-And, take it easy on your first day out of the hospital.

-That kind of promise, I can't make. Okay, baby, go back to the ice. I gotta' check myself out.


Edward caught the train just as it was pulling into the station and got himself a seat. He put his duffel bag on his lap and browsed through the newspaper. A news item on page 16 was interesting: there was an attempted suicide last month on an elevated train line near Highland Park: the night of his visit to his father's grave. The man had sustained serious injuries and, initially, medics thought he had expired from those injuries. Foul play was suspected, but the man would not cooperate with the authorities. He was transferred to Wyckoff hospital in critical condition. Witnesses are being sought in the case, but no one as yet has come forward.

-What the hell is that all about? What's there to investigate? Attempted murders happens every day in this city. If the guy doesn't want an investigation, it could mean that he knew his attacker. It could be a gangland hit. He's probably scared to name his attacker.

Edward read on: the man was no longer listed in critical condition and his nearest relative, his daughter, would not make any comment either to the authorities or the press.

-A tight fisted family. It's gotta' be gang related or even Mafia.

He got off at his stop on Fulton St. and headed on up to his office on the 10th floor. The elevator door was opened by a new lift man: a young man in his late teens.

-Good morning. Edward Mendez.

-Nice to meet you, Mr. Mendez. My name's Jack. Jack Marino.

-Welcome aboard, Jack. I've been out of commission for the past couple of weeks.

-I know. You're a hero, you know that? You pretty much saved the world.

-I had a lot of help.

-Thanks for the welcome and for what you did. I already met your sisters, Nella and Dottie Mendez. They're real nice. But, I may not be on the job for much longer.

-Why not?

-The owners are talking about putting in automated elevators. They want to modernize the building and cut costs.

-Don't worry about it, Jack. They might still find a place for you in maintenance.

-I sure hope so. I kinda' like working here.

-Keep me posted on what happens. I might be able to help.

Edward handed the young man a business card. He didn't have too many left. He made a mental note to have some more made up

-Thanks a lot, Mr. Mendez. I sure appreciate it.


Edward unlocked his office door. The phone was ringing. He slammed the door shut and reached for the receiver.

-Edward Mendez.

-Eddie? It's Dottie. I'm at the hospital. We just missed each other. Rotten luck.

-You didn't tell me you were coming. I would've waited.

-My fault. Anyway, Eddie?

He could tell that there was something wrong.

-What's up? Give. Don't be shy.

Dottie laughed.

-That, I'm not. I'll give it to you straight, handsome. I just might need your services as a Private Investigator. Can I come on over? You're not too busy, are you?

-Just got in. Come on over.

-I'll be there in fifteen minutes. Can I pick you up a pack of cigarettes?

-No, thanks. I've got my own.

Edward put the receiver down and looked about the dark office. No clients.

-Man, I'm gonna' have to drum up some business and fast.

There were two piles of mail on his desk. His sister Nella had been coming in these last few weeks along with Dottie and Yolanda to sort through his mail and keep the office tidy. Edward reached for the white, business envelope he knew to be the rent notice. He didn't open it. He knew his check balance was low and he wanted to postpone the inevitable.

\*\*\*

Marlena Lake was at her typewriter, the latest Underwood model, and she was just breaking it in. She pulled the sheet of paper out of the carriage and scanned it for any typographical errors. None. Good. She folded the paper, placed it in a business envelope and sealed it. She sat back in her chair, satisfied, and glanced out the window. It was a sunny day, but there was something in the air that made this woman uneasy. In spite of the brightness outside, there was an undertone of darkness...a darkness that even the sun's light couldn't quite dispel.

There was a knock on the study door and it startled Marlena out of her reverie.

-Come in, Susan.

Marlena's daughter entered. She was dressed to go out and was carrying some library books.

-Mother, I'm just going out to return some books to the library. Are there any errands you need doing?

-Yes. Mail this envelope for me, will you?

Susan took the envelope and glanced at the address.

-Mother?

-Yes, dear?

-Why are you writing to the Iranian embassy?

-Oh...no reason.

Susan didn't believe this for a second. She knew that her mother must be launching another one of her schemes; but, what had triggered it? Time would tell. The young girl left her mother's townhouse in a bemused state of mind. She didn't notice the man standing on the corner...the man who had been patiently waiting for her to come out.

***

Lt. Donovan was sitting in his own office at police HQ over on 86th St. on the upper east side of Manhattan. His desk had several sheets of paper on it: one for each victim, that is, for each known victim. Were there more rotted corpses to be found? It was a big city and Lt. William Donovan suspected that there were more victims. Sgt, Rayno, who was sitting opposite the Lieutenant, had that same disturbing thought. The Sergeant was facing the window and, like Marlena Lake, he, too, felt the darkness despite the sun.

-Let's go through this, again, Sergeant.

He handed over the sheets of paper to Sgt. Rayno.

The first victim had been a man known to both the Lieutenant and the Sergeant: Mr. Wulf Holderman: a known Nazi who was wanted for further questioning involving last month's disappearance of the sun. He'd been found in the back room of his book shop on 18th St. just off of 5th Ave. There was no sign of a break-in and nothing, as far as authorities could tell, had been taken from the shop.

The second victim had been a young man whose body was found stuffed in a garbage can outside of a bar frequented by homosexuals in the SoHo district of Manhattan. A pan handler had been doing the rounds and discovered the body. No clues. No witnesses. And, once again, a barely recognizable body.

Lt. Donovan started reading from his own copy.

-There were three other victims, Rayno: a business-man was found rotting away in a restroom stall at Grand Central Station. The corpse was stinking up the room so the attendant went to investigate. He nearly went hysterical when he got the door open.

The Lieutenant took a deep breath and continued,

-Then, there was a young Asian waiter found out-side the restaurant where he worked on Broome St. It was just after Christmas when the body was spotted in an alleyway by a patrolman on duty. The victim's clothes were intact, but Mr. Martin Ho was barely recognizable as a human being. We got the poor slob's name from his wallet. He was a hard worker and just recently married. He was also studying accounting at night school.

Lt. Donovan heaved a sigh.

-And, the last victim was found in the middle of the street pretty near to where the Asian waiter was found. A passing motorist nearly ran over it. Her body wasn't as badly decomposed as the others. The medics are trying to figure out why not. No witnesses. No clues. That last victim's name was Adele Locke, a waitress at MacDougall's Cafe in the West Village. Her handbag was found next to the body; that's how we I.D.ed her so fast

Sgt. Rayno waited for his superior to speak. He didn't have long to wait.

-Well, Sergeant, our serial killer favors Manhattan proper, but...and this is key…why Manhattan?

Sgt Rayno sat there looking at a man he admired. A man who had undergone a dramatic change of character over the last few weeks. Lt. Donovan had been a police officer who was thorough and tough and, sometimes, brutal. He was dogmatic and could be downright invasive in his interrogations. And, he usually got his man. But, last month's traumatic episode of the sun's disappearance had changed him and his methods.

Instead of doggedly following procedure, he now was determined to thwart the  rule book and damn the torpedoes. He was now what Sgt Rayno thought he'd never be: a rule breaker and unpredictable.

Lt. Lieutenant continued,

-Wulf Holderman was a person of interest in the sun's disappearance. He's dead and more than one person oughta' take a big interest in that: one person in particular.

-Who did you have in mind, Lieutenant.

-Edward Mendez, Private Investigator.

-Why Edward Mendez? I mean, I like the guy and all, but-

Lt. Donovan's smile was downright nasty.

-I've got a folder on Edward Mendez, P. I. He's an interesting man with a few well kept secrets. As it happens, a sister of his, Dorothy Mendez, lived in the Bushwick section of Brooklyn, pretty much a working class neighborhood. Well, a few weeks ago, right before Wulf Holderman's body was found, a teenager by the name of Angel Ulysses Correa went missing. His parents reported it to their precinct with the help of a Miss Dottie Mendez. I got wind of it from a friend of mine down there.

-The same day we think Wulf Holderman was killed? Did the boy go missing during the sun's disappearance? He could just have left home or even taken his own life. There were more than a few suicides back then.

-Maybe. He went missing on the day the sun reappeared. He was spotted leaving his house that morning and hasn't been seen since. And, as you know, I don't believe in coincidence. And, man, is it cold in here!

Lt. Donovan turned his chair around to face the radiator.

-Heat's not coming up.

The Lieutenant glanced out the window.

-Is it my imagination, Rayno-  forget it. We're just not getting the direct rays of the sun. That must be it.

Sgt. Rayno nodded.

-So, Mendez's sister is how we get in on this case?

-Just about. You look a little skeptical, Sergeant.

-Not really. But, maybe the sister already tipped Mendez off.

-That's what I'm hoping for. Mendez is suppose to be getting out of the hospital today. I'm putting a tail on him...namely, you.

***

Dottie Mendez made herself comfortable in the straight back, wooden chair that faced her brother's desk. She placed her black pocketbook on the floor, but not before she took out a fresh pack of cigarettes. She offered one to Edward.

-Got my own, sis. Lucky Strikes. But, thanks.

-I'm a Camel's girl myself: nice, strong flavor that sticks to the tongue.

-Too strong for me. Here. Use this ashtray. So, what's up?

-I might have a client for you.

-Keep talking. I need one real bad.

Dottie took a deep drag on her cigarette.

-It's like this; a young boy who lived across the hall from me took a powder a couple of weeks back. Can't give you an exact date, but it was just around the time that the sun popped back into view.

Dottie gave out a nervous laugh.

-And, that's pretty much it. I know! It sounds like nothing.

-Tell me about the boy.

-His name's Angel Correa. He's about nineteen and maybe around five foot seven, but gives the impression of being taller. He's a bodybuilder and a loner and handsome in an unusual sort of way..

-Be a little more specific. Try.

-Large, piercing brown eyes, arched eyebrows, a full mouth and a strong jaw. He keeps his hair close cropped – never lets it grow.

-You'd notice him in a crowd?

-Oh, yes. Couldn't miss him.

-Did he, maybe, just run away from home?

-Not the type. He's devoted to his father who's a bricklayer. His mom's a housewife and a little on the brusque side. And...he's not the social type. Doesn't make friends that easily.

-So, he'd have a hard time in a new setting.

-I think he would, Eddie.

-How well do you know this muscle man? And, what gymnasium does he work out of?

-I don't know him that well at all. But, the one time that we did have a conversation....it was a damned interesting one.

-His work out gym? Where is it?

-I think...yes! Sullivan's Gymnasium.

-I know where it is. A buddy of mine used to be a member there. Now tell me about your conversation with him.

-It's how it ended, that's the kicker.

Edward put out his cigarette.

-Okay. Start from the end.

-We were just about to part ways going to work-

-You okay, sis?

Dottie had to take a deep breath.

-No. I'm not okay, Eddie. Just thinking about it...and that look in his eye. He told me that when he was in the hallway that night, he was deciding whether or not to kill me.

Edward leaned forward in his chair, took out a cigarette and lit up. The steam pipes started clanging which meant the heat was coming up.

-Okay, listen up: take out another cigarette and tell me every damned thing you know about Mr. Angel Correa. Has he got a middle name, by the way?

-Ulysses.

Edward let out a long stream of cigarette smoke. The newspaper that he'd read that morning flashed in his mind.

-I don't know how long I can sit on this; but, I think we just might have a lead on the serial killer the police have been hunting for.

The P. I. tapped some cigarette ash into the glass ashtray.

-Eddie, you can't be serious.

-My P. I. gut is always serious. Now, all we've got to do is find the bastard.

***

Susan hailed a taxi cab. She gave instructions to the driver to head for midtown at 42 St. and 5th Ave. where the main branch of the public library was located. She was returning some books that she'd taken out as per her mother's instructions on the day of the infamous blackout. She shuddered just thinking about it. The newspapers still carried stories about the phenomenon that had almost extinguished life on the planet. Theories abounded and a certain level of fear lingered in the air. Would the underground Nazis try again or were they frozen alive down in Antarctica? The military had sent an expedition to the bottom of the world to find out. Did Susan's mother have any answers? Miss Lake didn't seem the least bit concerned. Susan smiled. Her mother probably had new fish to fry.

The cab dropped Susan off right in front of the main entrance. She did notice how nice of a day it was: sunny, crisp and a touch of wind to give it just that nip of winter. But, the cold was penetrating. Was she coming down with a cold?

Gerard Denza

Another cab pulled up in the same spot as Susan's cab. A man climbed out and approached her.

-Good morning, Miss Broder. My name is Turhan Aswan. You do not know me; but, I know of you.

Susan was taken aback by this handsome and dapper man. She was also curious. She stuffed her handkerchief back into the pocket of her trench coat.

-How is it that you know me, Mr. Aswan?

-Through your many articles on metaphysics and philosophy. I am a man, Miss Broder, whose trade is death.

-Come again?

-Perhaps, we could enter that modern coffee shop across the street? I have much to tell you and even more to ask of you and your mother, Miss Marlena Lake.

-Have you had us investigated, Mr. Aswan? It sure sounds like it.

-Yes. Weren't expecting such a direct answer, were you?

-Frankly, no.

-I like surprising people. And, now, shall we proceed to the coffee shop? It's rather cold.

Susan smiled in spite of herself.

-I'm game. But, I must return these books first. One more day and they'll be overdue.

-Of course. I will accompany you.

\*\*\*

Edward Mendez was headed to the Bushwick section of Brooklyn. He had dropped off his sister at their mom's place in Park Slope. She moved back in only a couple of weeks ago with her new cat.

He went in with Dottie to say hello to his mother and two other sisters: Nella and Victoria. He reassured them that he was perfectly fine and ready to work. It's what he needed to do. No one argued with their kid brother.

And, that's when Edward spotted Stripes: the tabby cat Dottie had rescued. He was staring up at Edward wit his big, green eyes. Edward picked him up and stroked him.

-Cute little fellow. How ya' doing, pal? You keeping these ladies in line? You're the man of the house, you know.

Dottie was beaming with pride.

-Isn't he adorable? And, friendly, too. We all love him to death even mother.

Edward handed Stripes over to her.

-He's a winner. By the way, where's the resident matriarch?

-Taking her late morning nap. You're safe enough, brother.

-Give her my regards. And, tell her I'll try to drop by soon.

-Come to dinner next week and bring Yolanda if she can make it.

-I'll ask her. Gotta' go. I've got some leg work to do.

-Want me to come along, Eddie? I know Angel's parents and, besides, I'm out of a job. Got myself fired.

-You don't look too broken up about it.

-I'm not. Good riddance to the place. I'm waiting for my first unemployment check.

-Not this time…maybe next time.

-Oh, be a sport. Why not? It'll give me an excuse not to look for work.

-One person is just a nuisance; but two people would be intimidating. But, I'll tell you what you can do: phone Yolanda's ice rink – I'll give you the number. I spoke with her just before leaving the hospital. Tell her to stay put until I pick her up at about five. And, tell her not to talk to strangers and to stay in someone's company at all times.

Dottie laughed and put Stripes down on the sofa.

-I think I've got all that. And, I've got the rink's phone number.

-Good.

-And, don't worry. I'll keep trying until I get through. Now, get moving, kid brother, and keep me posted.

Edward kissed Dottie on the cheek and said good-bye.

Edward found a parking space in front of Dottie's old apartment building. He'd driven down the one way street just behind the local bus that ran the circuit from downtown Brooklyn to the Myrtle and Wyckoff Ave. subway. There were only a few people about, mostly housewives on their way to grocery shopping or running a local errand.

The P. I. got out of his car and locked up. He took a deep breath of fresh air and stopped himself from taking out a cigarette. He had potential clients to see and they might not appreciate his smoking...some people didn't.

He climbed the few steps of the stoop, opened the outer vestibule door and ran his index finger along the metal mailboxes. Dottie's name was still listed.

-I guess they haven't had time to rent out her apartment.

The name "Correa" was next to "Dottie Mendez." Edward pushed the button and waited. He was buzzed in almost immediately. He pushed open the door and walked straight to the stairwell. It was dark in the corridor. He climbed the stairs and reached the first landing.

He knocked on the door opposite his sister's old place. He could hear footsteps walking toward him from behind the door. The door was opened by an attractive, middle-aged woman. The expression on her face was not pleasant

-Yes? May I help you?

-My name is Edward Mendez, Mrs. Correa.

-You must be Dottie's younger brother. Please, come in. We've been expecting you.

Edward walked in and waited for Mrs. Correa to close the door.

-Come into the living room; my husband's in there. I know he wants to talk to you.

The P. I. followed Mrs. Correa into a small and brightly lit room where a handsome man of about forty-five was sitting in an easy chair. He got up to shake hands with Edward, whose first thought kind of surprised him.

-Angel looks like his dad.

-Please, sit down, Mr. Mendez.

Edward sat on the sofa next to Mrs. Correa.

-Would you mind if I smoked?

Mr. Correa answered.

-No  Go right ahead. And, if you could spare one?

-You bet.

Edward flipped him a cigarette.

-Mr. Correa? Mrs. Correa? You must know that I'm a private investigator. Your son, Angel, has gone missing.

Edward was careful not to mention his theory about their son being a serial killer. To tell the truth, he wasn't certain and he had no proof to back up his theory...so why upset these people?

Mrs. Correa spoke up.

-That's true, Mr. Mendez. Angel went missing the day the sun reappeared in the sky. I remember how happy we were. We waited for Angel to come home from the gymnasium, which happens to be his second home. But, he never did. My husband was upset; but, I was angry with him. I'll admit that.

Edward nodded and looked around for an ashtray. Mr. Correa handed him a small metal one.

-Here you go.

-Thanks.

Edward's next question surprised even him.

-Was your son unhappy?

Mr. Correa answered the P. I.

-Yes. But, not so unhappy that he would run away from home. Everything he earned at the gymnasium or from modeling he gave to us. He only took for himself the daily expenses and his bodybuilding needs. He's a good boy and responsible.

Mr. Correa was holding back something.

-Did Angel have a girlfriend?

-Yes. Some tramp he met in the hospital. He brought her around once. Didn't like her.

That was Mrs. Correa being completely honest.

-What was her name?

-Valerie, Mr. Mendez. She really wasn't Angel's type. I can't think of her last name. I don't think he knew the girl all that well.

-She liked him more than our son liked her. She was after something and I don't know what. Excuse me, please.

And, with that, Mrs. Correa left the room to go into the kitchen.

-Mr. Mendez, please call me Hector. And, now we can talk more freely. Let me tell you about my son. He's a dedicated bodybuilder and pretty much a loner. He had only one close friend, Jaime Morillo, a nice boy. The two of them were close, if you get my drift. I'm not blind to these things. Young boys go through this phase.

-But, Angel wasn't that close to this girl, Valerie?

-I liked the girl, but there was something about her I didn't trust. You might want to track her down. She might know where Angel is.

Was Mr. Correa hinting at something? Maybe.

-Hector, I was led to believe you were incapacitated.

-For a short time, I had to get around on crutches. I work in construction and had an accident and had to take it easy for awhile. As a matter of fact, that's how Angel met Valerie; in the hospital while visiting me. Her father was in the other bed. He was bandaged from head to foot with third degree burns over most of his body. At least, that's what I assumed. I heard that he wasn't expected to live.

-Christ! Pretty rotten way to die.

-Yes. I never found out the cause of the accident, but...

Edward tapped some cigarette ash into the metal ashtray.

-But, what, Hector? Give.

-His daughter was so detached. There was no concern or compassion in her manner; at least none that I noticed. She was annoyed at just being there and that's when she latched on to Angel. And, that's when he started to change. Up until then, he was pretty content with his life, at least, most of the time.

-A woman can change a man, and sometimes not for the better.

-Don't I know it.

The two men shared a good laugh, but only for a moment.

-Mr. Mendez?

-Edward.

-Edward, do you think my son is dead or-  I can't bring myself to say it.

-I want you to say it, Hector.

Mr. Correa's hands were shaking.

-I can't!

The P. I. wanted to spare Mr. Correa his dark suspicions about his son, but he knew that he couldn't.

-I'll be up front. Angel could be one of our serial killer's victims or he could have decided to duck out of town for a few days with his girlfriend. Or...he could even be our serial killer — which is a long shot.

-No! I can't believe that. He'd be better off dead.

-It's only a suspicion. I shouldn't have said anything. Let me find out, Hector. It's better to know. My sister, Dottie, filled me in on some of the details.

-Your sister's a nice lady. She pretends to be tough, but she's soft-hearted.

-You've got her number, all right.

-Edward, please find my Angel. Your sister mentioned a fee of three hundred dollars plus expenses. Can you start right away?

-I'll start right now.

Mr. Correa called out to his wife in the kitchen.

-Louisa, bring in my checkbook, please.

Edward sat back in the armchair and lit another cigarette.

-First thing I'm gonna' do is track down this Valerie chick. What hospital were you staying in, Hector?

-Wyckoff Hospital. It's only a ten minute walk from here.

-Good. That's a starting point.

Edward pocketed the personal check for $300. He wasn't going to charge them for daily expenses.


Edward Mendez walked out of Wyckoff Hospital putting his notepad back in his jacket pocket. The red brick building dated back to the the late 1890's and was in need of repair; but, the staff made a good impression on the P. I. They were courteous and had tried to be helpful. The head nurse remembered Henry Vandor and his daughter. The father was okay, but the daughter was another matter. She hadn't been at all friendly and rarely talked to any of the staff.

Edward zipped up his jacket. The day was getting colder despite the sun's warmth. He put his scarf back on, but not his gloves. He leaned against his Ford. Henry Vandor had been checked out of the hospital...alive. His daughter had signed the release papers and had him transferred to a private sanatorium...a sanatorium that didn't exist. Edward had an address for the "sanatorium" and another one for Valerie Vandor: 418 Stanhope Street. He got in his car and drove straight there.

The sun disappeared behind some clouds. Was it Edward's imagination or could he feel the temperature drop?

The P. I. found a parking space just a couple of blocks from the Vandor address. He walked over to the building which was right next to the elevated train line. No "Vandor" was listed on the mail boxes.

-Why am I not surprised?

He rang the Super's bell, who turned out to be the landlady, and was buzzed in. The hallway was dark and smelled of cheap perfume. The Super was waiting for him inside her doorway: a tall and broad woman wearing a cobbler apron.

-What can I do for you?

Edward smiled and took off his hat.

-Name's Edward Mendez. I'm looking for a Miss Valerie Vandor.

-Moved out, doll, weeks ago.

-Did she leave a forwarding address?

-You her boyfriend?

-No. I knew her father. Thought I'd look him up.

-Then, why'd you ask for her? You're not some kind of private dick, are you? I can spot 'em from a mile.

-You're sharp.

-That's what they tell me. And, to answer your question: no. She didn't leave no forwarding address. And, her old man didn't live here either. Least-way, I never saw him.

-When did Valerie move out?

-A couple of days after the sun made a return trip. Her rent was all paid up, so I couldn't hold nothing against her.

-What kind of a girl was she?

By this time, Edward assumed the woman was not asking him inside of her apartment. He leaned against the wall.

-The bohemian type, if you know what I mean: dressed like a man, but she could get away with it. The Greenwich Village type. What the hell she was doing in this dump, beats the hell out of me. It really wasn't her kind of neighborhood. But, she kept to herself and kept the noise down when her muscle bound boyfriend showed up.

-Did you catch the boyfriend's name?

-Angel. Couldn't tell you the last name 'cause I never knew it.

-What's your name, by the way?

-Tess.

-Tess, by the way, did anyone else visit her?

-Now that you mention it, no. Kind of strange that with her being so young and attractive...not really pretty, mind you.

-What about her?

-What about her?

-What did you really think of her, Tess. Give.

-She was nice, but too quiet. Not shy, mind you. It was like she was being careful not to give out too much, if you know what I mean.

-This boyfriend, Angel, what about him?

-The silent, brooding type. You could tell that he was really feelin' the cold when the sun disappeared like it did. Came in with a container of steaming coffee and gulps it right down. And, the dirty look he give me one time.

-What kind of a look?

-Like he was fixing to kill me or somethin' worse.

-Did Valerie leave anything behind?

-Just a few feminine things. Nothing to jot down in your notebook, doll.

-Here's my card. If you remember anything else, call me. I've got an answering service.


Edward drove into Manhattan and headed straight for Sullivan's Gymnasium. It took him awhile to find a parking space; but, he managed to get one a few blocks away. The sun was giving way to clouds, one could feel the cold winter dampness in the air. And, Edward lectured himself.

-Angel Ulysses Correa is a serial killer: that's pretty close to a fact. And, why the hell am I so damned sure about that? Instinct? Wishful thinking that I lucked out on to the right suspect? God only knows.

Edward put his Fedora on.

-What could've pushed him over the edge? A girl-friend? A frustrated ambition? Pent up hatred at the world? He had only one close buddy and one girlfriend...a handsome bodybuilder like that. If I knew his motives, will that help me find him? Do I go to the cops with what I know? I'd better do that and real soon.

Edward threw his cigarette into the street and let himself into the gymnasium. The front desk was to his left and there was a staircase straight ahead, and just past the front desk was a door that led into the locker room. The gymnasium took up three floors in addition to a shower room and steam room in the basement.

A young and well-built man was tending the front desk. He was wearing a white tank top and sweat pants.

-Can I help you?

Edward took off his Fedora and smiled at the young man.

-Name's Edward Mendez and I'll get straight to the point. I'm a private investigator.

The young man behind the counter grinned.

-Looking for Angel Correa?

Edward tried not to show his surprise.

-As a matter of fact, I am. And, you're a couple of steps ahead of me, pal.

-I didn't like him. Too quiet and too much to himself and his buddy, Jaime Morillo. There was talk about those two. They were an item.

-When did you last see them?

-Last saw Correa around Christmas or maybe a few days later. I can check the log-in sheet, if you like.

-I'd appreciate that. By the way, you got a name?

-Randy Bates.

-What about Jaime Morillo?

-They stopped coming at about the same time. But, now that I think of it, they started "missing" each other. That was strange.

-Maybe they joined another gymnasium.

-Maybe. But, they'd be hard pressed to find a cheaper one.

The young man bent down behind the counter and came up with a thick ledger book. He flipped it open.

-Here it is. It was the 22nd of last month.

-You found that real fast. Thanks.

-That's according to this log, Mr. Mendez. Sometimes, especially in the morning, members just walk in without bothering to sign-in. We've been short staffed these past few weeks with the sun disappearing and all. We're just getting ourselves organized.

-I understand, Randy.

-And, a cop was here last week asking me the same questions that you're asking. What are you smiling about?

-What was this cop's name? I just might know him.

-I've got his card. Here it is. Lt. Donovan. He wasn't as nice as you are.

Edward took a good long look at the Lieutenant's card. He handed it back to the young man.

-Here's my card, Randy. If Angel should show up, call me like, pronto.

-Why? What's up with Correa? Got himself in trouble?

The question had an arrogant tone.

-Why? Because he might be a murderer. Better stay clear of him.

Edward drove into Chinatown. He'd put a scare into the young man back at the gym. Would Lt. Donovan have approved? He didn't give a good crap. The P. I. still hadn't forgiven him for his subterfuge a few weeks back. Yes. Edward held grudges. And, why not? He didn't like being lied to and played for a chump. So.Donovan was on the case. He smiled.

-Okay, pal, if you're looking to rankle me, you can just forget it. I don't rankle so easy. Bastard! Irish, fucking bastard!

Edward ran the next red light.

# Chapter Two
# January 4,1948  P.M.

IN MIDTOWN Manhattan, at the main branch of the post office on 8th Avenue between 31st and 33rd Streets, a young German girl of nineteen stood on the steps of that impressive building. The architecture was inspired from ancient Rome with massive stone columns supporting the building's facade.

Eva Ceres had to stop looking upward or she would strain her pretty neck. The tall girl began climbing those steps with the intention of mailing a small package to her parents back in Leipzig, Germany. The package contained two gold wedding rings: an anniversary present for her parents. She hadn't seen them in over

two years because of the war and her attending university at Hunter College for nursing.

Eva made it up the steps and entered the building,
but just before opening the glass door, she spotted a
young man coming up the stairs right behind her.
Should she open the door for him? Why not? She did
and smiled at the young man who now hurried up the
remaining steps. He was unusual looking, but striking:
large, almond shaped eyes behind the clear, wire-
rimmed spectacles. He sported close-cropped hair and
one could see that he frequented the gymnasium. Eva
approved of the fine specimen.

-I wonder if he's as nice as he looks?

Eva released the door, smiled at the young man and
walked over to one of the counters to check over her
package and fill out the proper forms for mailing it. She
glanced at herself in the window's reflection: her long,
dark hair was securely pinned in place and she felt that
her makeup didn't need any retouching.

Eva walked over to where people were queued up
for a postal worker; that same young man was headed in
her direction. She showed off her package to him.

-Not bad, no?

-Looks pretty good. You can get ahead of me, if you
like. I'm in no hurry.

Eva noted the Latin accent.

-Thank you so much. You very sweet.

The line of people moved quickly and Eva reached window three. The woman behind the counter advised Eva to put some more glue on one of the folds of the package. She did, but the cap came off and she knocked the bottle over to prevent the glue from spilling all over her. The woman behind the counter was irate.

-Oh, for heaven's sake! I just cleaned that counter. Look at the mess you made, young lady.

-I had to do that or it would have spilled all over me. What would you have me do?

The woman didn't answer. Instead, she grabbed the package, posted it and threw it into the appropriate bin. Eva walked away from the window more than a little embarrassed.

The young man approached her.

-I saw what happened. You ticked her off real good.

-Oh! You still here? Yes. She was nasty, wasn't she?

-It was an accident. I'll walk with you down the stairs, if you don't mind.

The postal agent was still glaring at Eva and noticing the young man who was obviously her boyfriend. Ellen Barnett was the last person to see Eve Ceres alive. A body would be found in a back alley in Chinatown; at least, something that had once been a human being. The remains would never be identified. Eva would be listed as "missing: whereabouts unknown." Her parents would receive their daughter's anniversary present.

\*\*\*

Edward Mendez was smoking in the reception area of Mr. Aswan Turhan's funeral parlor. It was the address of the "sanatorium" that Valerie Vandor had given to Wyckoff Hospital. The P. I. had been told to wait for Mr. Aswan by a petite and soft spoken woman.. He was surprised when a familiar figure emerged from the ladies room. He got to his feet.

-Susan! What the hell are you doing here? This can't be a coincidence.

Susan laughed and gave Edward a hug.

-That's a difficult question to answer. We may be part of a Domino Effect. But, wait a minute. How are you? I was going to visit you in the hospital today. You saved me a trip downtown. How gallant.

-I'm okay. Vision is a little sharper than usual, but I'm not complaining. Decided to check myself out a day earlier, that's about the size of it. I'm the restless sort.

And, now, young lady, back to this "Domino Effect." It wouldn't-

-Have anything to do with my mother? Of course it would. She's the master manipulator; that is, when her schemes aren't backfiring on her. And, by the way, shamus, what are you doing here? Not planning any-one's funeral, I hope.

Edward laughed.

-Nope. Not even my own. I'm here to see the head man of this joint.

-What in the world for? My mother didn't send you here, did she?

-She didn't.

-Edward, I'd love to stay and chat; but, I have a cou-ple of more errands to run.. Can you drop by our place this evening for a late dinner? And, bring Yolanda if she can make it.

Susan Broder had no romantic designs on Edward Mendez.

-I'll try, but don't hold me to a promise.

-I won't. And, take care not to over do it on your first day out of the hospital.

The moment Susan left, Mr. Aswan made his ap-pearance. He was a handsome man of medium build and height. He sported one of those pencil mustaches that Edward didn't care for. His black, three piece suit looked expensive and well cut. The tie was silk and the shirt was made of Egyptian cotton.

Mr. Turhan Aswan extended his hand to the P. I.

-Mr. Mendez? A pleasure to meet you. To what do I owe the honor?

Edward had a plausible story for his visit all ready.

-A friend of mine was here a couple of weeks ago: Mr. Henry Vandor. His wake was held here.

-I see. And, how may I help you?

-Is there a record of who attended the wake? I think we might have had some friends in common. You see, Mr. Aswan, I couldn't make it to the funeral. I was in the hospital and just got out today.

-The ledger would be with his family. I'm afraid that I can't help you.

-He had a daughter named Valerie.

-Did he, indeed? I don't recall who attended.

Edward took note of Mr. Aswan's petulant manner.

-Of course not. You're a busy man, Mr. Aswan.

And, an ill-mannered bastard. Edward could see that the undertaker had no intention of inviting him into his office or even offering him a seat. But, Edward wasn't so easily put off.

-Would you have a forwarding address for the daughter? She  seems to have moved since her dad's wake and I would like to get in touch with her.

-I couldn't give you that kind of information even if I had it. It would come under client confidentiality, you know.

-Why your funeral parlor, pal?

-I beg your pardon?

The veil of civility had now been dropped by both men.

-You heard me. Why here in Manhattan, when Vandor died in Brooklyn?

-Find his daughter and ask her. I don't question my clients. And, I certainly don't turn down business.

-I'm asking you. He cashes in his chips in Brooklyn and the daughter brings him here. That doesn't make too much sense. And, by the way, Mr. Aswan, when Vandor's daughter checked him out of the hospital, he was alive and this place was listed as a sanatorium. What gives? Why did his daughter lie about where her father was going?

-I don't know how to answer your questions. You've taken up enough of my time.

-Have it your way. But, I've got my eye on you, pal. Edward put his Fedora back on.

-Be seeing you, Mr. Aswan.

The P. I. turned his back on the undertaker and walked out.


It was close to four o'clock and Edward realized that he hadn't eaten since leaving the hospital that morning. The day was now overcast and the temperature was dropping. He drove through Chinatown and headed toward Chambers St. and Park Place.

He parked his car only a few spaces from Nedicks which was a sort of eat-and-run place. He got himself their famous orange drink and a couple of frankfurters. His girlfriend, Yolanda, wouldn't approve, but he was hungry and wanted to make fast tracks to his office on Fulton St. and Broadway. He asked for a lid for the container and got back in his car.

And, in a few minutes, he was in his office on the tenth floor sorting through two piles of mail: business and personal. It was close to five o'clock when his phone rang.

-Edward Mendez.

-Hello, doll, it's Tess from Stanhope St. You haven't forgotten me, have you? It usually takes a day and a half.

The P. I. was surprised. He hadn't expected to hear from the landlady so soon...if at all. He knew how to handle this type of chick.

-Tess, baby, I sure do remember you. So, you didn't throw my card into the garbage can after all.

-Now, would I go and do a thing like that?

-What gives, baby?

-Well, it's like something out of one of those Sherlock Holmes movies. That tenant who took over Valerie's apartment? Well, she's been wanting a paint job done and the wallpaper that's in there has got to come off.

-Okay, so what did she come across?

-You're sharp, doll. She was peeling off the old paper from the bottom up and notices this notepaper stuck on the the back of the wallpaper so she tries taking it off. It won't come off, so she cuts the wallpaper around it and brings it down to me to have a look at. Can't make heads or tails out of it.

-What was on it?

-Some kind of scrawl like one of those ancient languages; but, it wasn't Greek or Hieroglyphics. I'd have recognized them. I go to the movies, you know.

-Mind if I drive by, say tomorrow morning, to have a look?

-Wouldn't mind at all, handsome, but it's not here anymore.

Edward's voice took on a sharp edge.

-Why not, Tess. Give.

-Don't get mad at me.

-Just tell me what you did with it.

-My nephew, who's a teacher at Hunter College, well, he come by this afternoon for a visit and to bum a free meal. So, I show it to him. And, what do you think? He knew what it was...well, sort of.

-Don't keep me suspense, Tess. What did he say it was?

-He said it was the first written language ever: cuneiform  The ancient Sumerians invented it thousands of years ago.

Sumer: the first known civilization. Edward stared straight ahead at the frosted panel on his office door. For the second time that day, he had an uneasy feeling in his P. I. gut.

-Does your nephew read cuneiform?

Tess laughed.

-Hell, no. But, a buddy of his in college does. So he took it with him to be translated into English.

-Tess, tell me your nephew's name and who is this friend of his?

-I gotta' think for a second. Well, my nephew's Herbert Adams and like I say, he teaches at Hunter.

-And, his friend?

-He said it. Must be getting old- got it! Name's Daniel Gifford. He teaches ancient history.

Edward had his notepad out and was jotting down these names when he heard a "click" on the phone line.

-Tess, did you hear that?

-I sure did. Are we on a party line or something, doll?

-Maybe.

-You think someone's been listening in? This is gettin' kinda' exciting.

-Listen, Tess, there's probably nothing to worry about, but go to your door right now and lock it and, then, go to every window in the place and do the same.

-Hey, you're starting to scare me.

-Just do as I say and come back to the phone.

-Hold on.

Edward didn't even think of taking out a cigarette.

-Hello? Tess! Tess?

-All locked up. I'm glad my old man's due home soon. Have I got a story to tell him.

-Good. That's good, Tess. And, don't let anyone you don't know in. Savvy?

-What's your next move, doll?

Edward grinned.

-I just might be taking a night class at Hunter College tomorrow night.

# Chapter Three
# January 5, 1948

PROFESSOR DANIEL Gifford's class on ancient Meso-
potamia started at 6 P. M. sharp and Edward didn't
want to be late. Edward Mendez called the school but
couldn't get a phone number for the professor or Tess's
nephew, Herbert Adams.

Edward had his jacket on and was reaching for his
Fedora when the phone rang. Christ! It was almost 5:30
and he had to get going. The trip out to Staten Island
had taken longer than expected. And, for what? To look
at the gutted remains of a building. There was nothing
there but burnt planks and a hole in the ground.

What had Marlena and Susan actually seen? The two
women were reliable enough and not prone to hysterics

or storytelling. No. Edward was certain that there had been a "house" which contained an unusual library. He had even seen and handled several of the books that Marlena and Susan had taken. It was puzzling because this demolished house had once been his father's occult HQ. The P. I. was certain of one thing however: that the house had been deliberately destroyed and its contents removed.

He picked up the phone. It might be important.

-Edward Mendez.

-Mr. Edward Mendez, Private Investigator? Have you forgotten about me?

-Yolanda! Oh, baby, I'm real sorry. I'm on my way. Give me just fifteen minutes. It's been one helluva' day.

He hung up. If he didn't run into traffic, he could pick up Yolanda at her ice rink in midtown and, then, head straight on up to Hunter. He switched off the overhead lights and locked up.


Traffic wasn't too bad heading uptown, so the P. I. made good time. The weather forecast had called for snow, but so far there was none in sight which suited Edward just fine. He didn't like New York snow. It started out pretty enough, but ended up in soot and slush.

Yolanda was waiting for him outside the main entrance to the ice rink with a duffel bag at her feet. Edward double parked his car, got out, kissed and embraced his girl and brought her and her duffel bag into his car.

-Baby, hold on tight. I've got some news for you.

-I'm pretty tired, Edward. Are we going straight home or out to dinner first?

-Later on both counts. We've got a lecture to attend at Hunter College. And, there's a couple of teachers who I need to talk to.

-Edward?

-What is it, baby? And, by the way, I like that perfume.

-I'm glad. It's a new fragrance I'm trying: Jungle Gardenia.

He stopped for a red light and leaned over to kiss Yolanda on the neck.

-Love it, baby. You're making me real hard.

-Then, this perfume was worth the money. But, love, I have to get up early tomorrow morning for practice. Would you mind dropping me off at my place? It's not too much out of your way. I have to practice my artistic program all day. I'm not looking forward to it, but I have to be on time.

-I'm sorry, baby, I forgot. I'll make a turn at the next corner and drop you off. I'll even go up with you and check out the place.. And, when I'm gone, don't let anybody in. I've got my own key, so I'll tiptoe on in later and try not to wake you up. And, remember, nobody but me gets in.

-Mmm. I knew there was a reason that I love you so.

It was nearly half past six o'clock when Edward arrived at the main entrance of Hunter College. It started snowing just a few minutes ago when he parked his car. He vaulted up the main staircase and scanned every room searching for the right one. Found it! Room 314.

He felt awkward just walking in, but he gritted his teeth, opened the classroom door and found himself an empty desk to sit behind. There were about forty students in attendance. He nodded to the instructor, Professor Gifford.

Edward took a deep breath. He wasn't listening much to the professor's words as he was observing some of the students. The P. I. had no way of knowing that one student was missing: Miss Eva Ceres. Her desk was empty, but her friend, Henriette Miller was there and was quite concerned about her missing friend. It was unlike Eva to miss class. And, why hadn't she called to let Henriette know that she wouldn't be coming to class tonight?

Henriette's concern showed in her face and her instructor had noticed it as he had noted Eva's absence. He was concerned, as well, but every student misses a class once in a while, don't they?

The lecture ended at around 8:30 P. M.

Professor Gifford noticed the two new faces in his class: both men. The one in the front row was pleasant looking enough, but the other one in the back row had kept his head down for most of the lecture. He didn't mind the extra faces because often students would drop in even though they weren't officially registered for his class.

The classroom was emptying out, but there were three stragglers: Edward, Henriette, and the man in the back row.

Henriette approached Professor Gifford's desk.

-Professor Gifford? I don't know what happened to Eva tonight. I tried reaching her, but she didn't pick up her phone. I'm a little worried. It's so unlike her. I know how she looks forward to your class.

Edward noted the German accent and the extreme politeness and respect that Henriette showed to her instructor. His impression of Henriette Miller was a good one. And, he almost laughed out loud at his next thought.

-I'll wager that she's Lt. Donovan's type of chick. I can even see them together.

Edward held back the laughter and waited to get the teacher's attention.

Professor Gifford smiled at his student. Henriette was, in fact, his favorite student: bright and eager and hanging on to his every word in class. The kind of student that every teacher dreamed of.

-Try her, again, when you get home. She's probably just feeling a bit under the weather.

-I hope so; but, with all these murders going on, I can't help but be worried.

Edward was also worried. The hairs on the back of his neck stood up.

-I understand. And, you, young lady, get home safely.

-I live only a few blocks away. I'll be fine, Professor Gifford.

-Try to walk home with someone. It's not safe walking the streets alone.

Professor Gifford turned to face Edward.

-May I help you?

-Edward Mendez. And, I won't take up much of your time, sir.

As Edward explained his reasons for being there, the man in the back row edged his way closer to the instructor's desk. Henriette was putting her books away in her satchel and getting ready to leave.

-A Mr. Herbert Adams might have given you an interesting and unusual document: one with cuneiform writing on it.

-How do you know this, Mr. Mendez? I've told no one.

-His aunt's tenant found it. She gave it to Mr. Adams' aunt who in turn gave it to him. Was that clear enough for you? I don't mean to sound abrupt; but, I'm real anxious to get a hold of this document.

-I see. I have taken a glance at it; but, not enough time for any real accurate translation. It seems to contain reference to scientific matter…astronomy, I think.

-Would it be possible to photostat it? I'd like the original document back. It could prove vital to an ongoing police investigation.

Henriette was about to leave when the man who had been sitting in the back row spoke up.

-Professor Gifford, I must speak with you in private...now, please.

Professor Gifford turned back to Edward.

-Would you excuse us for a moment?

Reluctantly, Edward acquiesced and followed Henriette out into the hallway. The P. I. took out a cigarette and offered one to the young girl. Henriette had her hair all done up in a "bun" and was still wearing her spectacles.

-Oh, no, thank you. I don't smoke.

-Do you mind if I smoke?

-Not at all.

He lit up.

-Who was that joker just now.

-I beg your pardon?

-The man who wanted to get rid of us.

-I've no idea. I've never seen him in class before. Did you notice how very furtive he was?

-I sure did. I'd like to know what the hell he's up to.

-Did you notice the-

Henriette didn't get a chance to finish her question as a piercing scream was heard from inside the classroom that she and Edward had just left. The young girl stepped away from the door in fear; but, Edward went to open the door. He couldn't. It was locked from the inside. The P. I. banged on the door.

-Professor! Professor Gifford! Are you all right?

The screams continued. And, then, Henriette screamed.

-My God! Mr. Mendez, it sounds as if he's being killed.

Edward backed away from the door and braced himself. A few students heard the screams and were rushing toward the classroom. Edward put all his weight behind his thrust at the locked door. The door flung inward; but, he was off balance and the man inside was able to rush past him and make good his escape down the hallway, shoving frightened students aside.

Edward struggled to steady himself as he took in the carnage: the instructor's desk had been overturned and there were papers scattered all over the floor. The professor lay on the floor face up. His face was smashed in and both arms were broken. His body was like that of a rag doll with its arms splayed and its torso disjointed. His neck had been broken.

The P. I. turned to close the door and seal the crime area. Henriette rushed in. She put her hands to her face and screamed.

-Oh, my God! He's been killed!

-You gotta' step out, Henriette, and get to the nearest phone and call the cops. Can you do that for me?

Henriette took a few deep breaths and brought her-self under control. The young girl nodded to Edward and rushed out of the classroom dropping her satchel to the floor. Students in the hallway were peering in so Edward closed the door and stayed in the room. As a professional, he knew better than to tamper with any-thing having to do with a crime scene.

He knew what had been taken. But, why not just grab the damned piece of paper and make a run for it? Why resort to a brutal murder that was sure to draw in the police? Edward knew why: the professor had translated enough of the document to get an idea of its import...ergo, eliminate him. Someone had listened in on his phone conversation with Tess...someone who knew he'd been at the landlady's place...someone who had followed him there.

# Chapter Four
# January 6, 1948

EDWARD LAY in bed next to Yolanda. He dozed off a couple of times but not for long. He had too many things on his mind. Where was Angel Correa hiding? Who tailed him yesterday and why hadn't he spotted the bastard? Was there a common thread to all these murders? There needn't be; sometimes, insane killers just pick an easy target.

And, then, the P. I's. mind shifted to recent past weeks. His sister, Catrina, was still in the hospital and was expected to recover. She had third degree burns over most of her body and would be scarred for life. However, the doctors were more concerned about her mental health than her physical condition. Catrina

Mendez had not uttered a word since regaining consciousness.

And, then, there was that house, or what was left of it, on Staten Island. Edward wanted to go out there again and investigate what remained of it. But, why? It bordered on an obsession.

Yolanda woke up with a start.

-Edward, I didn't hear you come in last night.

-I made sure that you didn't, baby. I was real quiet...just like a good cat burglar oughta' be.

He kissed her on the neck, inhaled her new perfume and filled her in on all the details of the previous day, including last night's murder.

-He had to kill the poor man for that?

Edward nodded and turned to look at the alarm clock on the night stand: 4:30 A.M. Like himself, his girlfriend kept crazy hours.

-It's funny, baby. If Angel Correa is our killer and, I'm pretty damned sure that he is, half of our problem is solved. Now, we just gotta' find the murdering bum.

-Who's "we?"

-Our "friend" Lt. Donovan's been nosing around.

-He's no friend, Edward. I'll bet he hasn't given up on Dolores' murder. Do you remember how he lied to us?

-We lied to him a few times, too. Albeit, we had to.

-That's different.

Edward laughed at the convenient double-standard. He looked around for his pack of cigarettes.

-It always is, baby.

-Looking for your cigarettes? Here they are.

She handed him his Lucky Strikes.

-Thanks. Want one?

-No, thanks. I'd better not. I'm in training. But, Edward, maybe someone is hiding Angel.

Edward lit up, inhaled and then exhaled.

-And, it's probably his good-for-nothing girlfriend, Valerie Vandor.

-Or a buddy of his. Maybe the man who killed that professor last night?

-He only had one buddy and that was Jaime Morillo who I still have to check out. And, who knows, maybe that Valerie chick is dead, too.

-For her sake, I hope not. Did Angel belong to any clubs, if you know what I'm hinting at.

-I think I know what you're getting at. But, the only club he belonged to was Sullivan's Gymnasium

-But, Edward, that man who killed the professor at Hunter last night...he must be involved somehow...and desperate.

-You know something, baby, you're still my Girl Friday. You're sharp. Mr. Angel Correa and his girlfriend are linked to some sleazy funeral parlor director who doesn't like answering questions.

Yolanda sat up in bed.

-They could all be part of some underground occult group. They're pretty dangerous, you know.

-I'd make bet on that.

-You might want to give Marlena a call. If this Mr. Aswan is part of an occult group, Marlena would know about it. She has connections all over the place.

-You're right. And, Susan was there yesterday.

-Then, Marlena must know something.

-That woman always knows something.

-Why would Susan visit a funeral parlor of all places?

Not waiting for a response, Yolanda got out of bed.

-I'll fix us some breakfast. And, Edward, you might want to talk with Angel's father, again. If his son changed or made new friends, he'd know; a father would know about that.

She went into the kitchen, but stopped short.

-And, another thing.

-I'm listening.

-I'll bet Lt. Donovan had you tailed yesterday. Don't trust him, Edward. And, who knows, maybe somebody was tailing the tail.

Edward refused the offer of a second cup of coffee. His sister, Dottie, raised an eyebrow and helped herself to a second cup of coffee and another slice of coffee cake. Stripes jumped on Edward's lap.

-How's mother these days?

-Her same, old self righteous and irascible self. She's sleeping in late, so you're safe enough.

Edward laughed and stroked Stripes under the chin.

-Dottie?

-Yes, Eddie?

-Did Angel Correa change in any way from his usual anti-social self?

-Now that you mention it, no. At least...well, I guess there was a sort of change in him. But, I didn't really know him all that well.

-Fill me in.

-His clothing. When I first moved in, he dressed kind of shabby...well, second hand clothes that were always clean, mind you. Then, he started sporting new clothes fresh off the rack.

-Keep talking.

-New pants and wing-tip shoes and a new gym bag; this was just a couple of days after the sun did a disappearing act. He even groomed himself a bit sharper. He was a good looking boy.

-So, he came into money. How?

-Maybe his bodybuilding started paying off. Maybe he started winning competitions. Maybe he rented himself out...you know...male escorts.

-You mean male prostitutes. Maybe. And, the last time you saw him?

-Late afternoon. I was on my way home from work. It was the day before the sun re-appeared. We were riding in the same subway car; but he didn't see me.

-Was he by himself?

-No. He was with some slick red-headed chick. Couldn't hear a word of what they were saying — very inconsiderate of them. Might've been Valerie.

-Had you seen this red head before?

-Nope. Didn't even know he had a girlfriend....and, yes!

Dottie almost dropped her coffee cup.

-His face. He had a sun tan, a gorgeous sun tan and not the kind you get from a sun lamp either. I know. I've tried 'em!

Edward lit another cigarette.

-New clothes. New girlfriend. And, maybe a quickie vacation in the tropics.

-So, shamus, what does it all add up to? I'm lousy at math.

-A new social circle.

-You just lost me.

-New and affluent friends, but-

Dottie leaned forward.

-Don't keep your favorite sister in suspense. Give!

-What price did Angel pay for all this?

\*\*\*

Miss Anna Chan was sweeping the debris from outside the front entrance of her thrift shop in Chinatown. Few people were out and about and those few were busy opening their own shops or stands. No one was paying any attention to the beautiful young woman who only a few weeks before had been sworn in as an American citizen. And, no one paid any attention to the young man who approached her.

-Excuse me?

-Yes?

Anna was taken aback by the young man's look, but only for a moment.

-May I help you? As you can see, I'm busy right now and my shop isn't yet open for business.

-You're about to sweep that trash into the street.

-And what business is that of yours?

-You don't know me.

-I do. You are the murderer. I know this. I don't know your name; but, I do know many things. I might even know what you are. I look into people's eyes. And, your eyes are the eyes of a murderer.

-You're not too smart for someone who knows a lot of things.

Anna looked him straight in the face.

-You don't scare me. You'd better come inside. People might overhear us and that's the last thing that we want.

-You're not scared that I just might kill you?

-I know how to defend myself. You wouldn't have such an easy time of it. And, I need your help.

-My help? What the hell can I do for you?

-I think I know how you came to be what you are. You're the man I've read about in the papers. You drain people of life.

Angel smiled and took off his ski cap.

-You know a little too much.

-Not enough. I want to know how you became what you are. You will share your secret with me. Here. Throw this trash in the street and, then, come in. I can offer you a safe hiding place.

# Chapter Five
# January 7, 1948

HENRIETTA WAS frantic with worry. Eva had not shown up at her apartment for close to two days. The young woman was still shaken from last night's drama and had gotten very little sleep.

Where could Eva be? Should Henriette call the police? Maybe, she should have told the police about her concern for her girlfriend last night. They had questioned her about Professor Gifford's murder, but there wasn't much that she could tell them. Mr. Mendez had been friendly enough, but just a little on the impersonal side. He had given Henriette his business card and she was looking at it right now. What could she tell the P. I.? Nothing. She didn't know anything.

Her thoughts went back to Eva: so very beautiful and popular with the boys, but not a flirt. She loved people and had a genuine concern for her friends' well being. She loved experimenting with different types of make-up and hairstyles and the latest fashion trends. Henriette had benefited from her cast off clothes and various cosmetics. Eva was a generous friend.

Where was Eva now?

Think, Henriette; use that logical German mind of yours and think! Did Eva spend the night with a boy-friend? Even if she did, which Henriette doubted, she would never have missed class. She was a straight "A" student who often studied late into the night.

Where had Eva been that afternoon? Where had she gone? What errands had she run? She'd taken a half day off from work and there had to be a good reason for that.

Henriette was late for work. She had a secretarial job at the United Nations that she certainly didn't want to jeopardize. Her fluency in German had gotten her the job along with her efficiency and pleasant manner. Quickly, she finished getting dressed and gathered up her pocketbook...and those letters on her nightstand had to be mailed-

-Of course! Eva went to the post office to send off her package to her parents. And, yes, it was the main post office on 31ˢᵗ St. She wanted to see the landmark building.

Henriette put down her pocketbook and picked up the phone. She dialed Edward Mendez's number.

-He will know what to do.

***

Edward knew what to do. Henriette told him approximately the time Eva had left for the post office.

-Next in line, please.

Edward walked up to the clerk behind window number four and showed his I. D.

-A private investigator, huh? How can I help you? We don't get many of those in here.

-A young, German girl was here three days ago, sometime in the early afternoon. She was very pretty and her name was Eva Ceres.

Edward showed the man the small photo that Henriette had given him.

-I'd have remembered her. Nice looking girl. She in some kind of trouble?

-Is there any way of checking who waited on her? Would you know off hand, by any chance?

-If it wasn't a special type of delivery-

-It was. She was sending off a small package to her folks in Leipzig, Germany and the items were valuable.

The man shook his head in the negative. From the corner of his eye, Edward saw that another employee had overheard their conversation. She was now motioning for the P. I. to come over to her window.

Edward thanked the man and walked over to window one.

-So, tall, dark and Latin, you're a private dick. Never met one in person, but I've seen a lot of them in the movies.

-Glad I'm the first. Just hope I'm making a good impression.

The woman laughed good-naturedly.

-I remember the girl you're looking for; spilled glue all over the counter here. Didn't mean to, I'm sure, but what a mess.

Edward nodded in appreciation of the woman's good memory.

-Did you send out the package?

-Sure. That's what I'm paid to do. She did a nice job of wrapping it, too. Odd last  name for a German girl:

"Ceres." Sounds more like Greek than anything else, don't you think?

That hadn't occurred to Edward.

-Next question.

-Ellen's the name.

-Ellen. Was she with anyone?

-No.

Damn it. Edward wanted to swear real bad, but didn't.

-Are you sure about that? Was any boyfriend waiting for her? Was anyone following her?

Ellen leaned across the counter and smiled.

-I was waiting for you to ask me that. A young man *did* leave with her. And, come to think of it, they even sorta' came in together. She held the door open for him. I'm a busybody. I notice these things.

Edward gripped the marble counter.

-And, they left together?

-Sure did. He even let her get ahead of him on line. Now, *that* practically never happens, I can tell you. He must have been on the make for her.

-Could you hear what they were saying to each other?

-Too far away for me to do my usual eavesdropping. Sorry.

-Ellen, what did this guy look like? Think, baby! This Eva chick may be in real trouble.

-Let me think. We get so many people coming in here. The girl, I remember. The boy wasn't tall...about your height. No offense.

-None taken. Keep talking.

-European look to him. Latin, like yourself. Can't swear to that. He was more striking than handsome, if you get my drift. You can tell he had a nice built under that bomber jacket of his.

-Was he carrying anything?

-I'd say, no. He carried himself like an athlete.

-See that? The more you talk, the more you're gonna' remember.

-He wore wire-rimmed spectacles; but, you didn't really notice them because of his look. So, is he your man, Mr. Mendez?

-I thought we were on a first name basis?

-Me on a first name basis with a private dick? Wait'll I tell the girls about this. They're gonna' die.

-And, to answer your question: he's my man all right.

Ellen stopped laughing.

-Hey, Edward, is that chick really in danger? I've been reading about these murders in the paper, lately. You're not telling me that he's the serial killer, are you?

Edward didn't want to frighten the woman.

-He's a suspect. And, I gotta' follow every lead.

-But, this girl...she could be dead. And, her being so young and pretty and all.

Edward's thought differed just a bit from that of the postal worker's.

-She's dead all right.

Edward turned around, after thanking Ellen, and caught sight of a man ducking behind one of the building's massive Roman columns. The P. I. shook his head and smiled  real broad like. He walked out of the building and on to the top step where last night's snow was turning to slush.

-Sgt. Rayno...Tom...good to see you, old boy.

The Sergeant stepped out from behind the column.

-Mendez. Good to see you, too. Sorry about all this cloak and dagger routine. Orders from above.

-I know. Orders straight from Lt. William Donovan. I think I'd like to pay the good Lieutenant a visit. He might even want to see me.


-Gentlemen, let's go through the list.

-In order of killing?

-You know how methodical I am, Mendez.

The Lieutenant paused to look at the sheet of paper in front of him. He and Edward were sitting in Lt. Donovan's small but neat office on East 86th St.

-And, by the way, Mendez, you knew one of these victims: Wulf Holderman. He was bumped off the day we brought you to Emergency.

-You've gotta' be kidding me.

-Nope. The Nazi bastard was the first victim we know of. And, if you want my opinion, he got what he deserved.

-If you're looking for an argument, Lieutenant, you better change the subject.

-Wulf Holderman indirectly links you — and, maybe, even me — to the case along with Correa and your sister knowing him.

Edward understood: connect the dots and you might get an image of a murderer.

-Okay. We've got rotted corpses: four of them. The question is: is that all?

Edward shook his head.

-I don't think so. A young girl, a student at Hunter College, has been missing for a couple of days which is why I was at the post office because that's the last place she was seen. And, we have a witness who says that she was with one, Angel Correa. They walked out of the building together.

-The teenager who's gone missing? We know about him. He's our serial killer? Don't tell me you've been holding out on me, Mendez. And, in the back of my head, i just might've had the same thought.

-Would I hold out on you, Lieutenant?

The three men in the office tried laughing, but didn't get too far.

-Anyway, I was hired by Correa's parents to find their son. He's nineteen and an aspiring bodybuilder. That young man who was found in a garbage bin in lower Manhattan might have been a fellow bodybuilder from Correa's gymnasium. I haven't had time to check on it.

-So, why kill him?

-That, I don't know. Maybe Correa found out that he couldn't trust him or maybe the bastard was just in a rotten mood or it might have been the random killing of a stranger. Maybe, the guy came on to Correa.

-And, what about the others? What about this student? Why does he go around killing people and leave the rotting corpse to be found?

-Maybe, he's new at the killing game. Couldn't tell you, Lieutenant. And, to be honest, I haven't got a damned piece of evidence against Correa: just circumstantial evidence and not too much of that. But-

-I'm listening.

-I've got this gut P. I. feeling that Correa's like some kind of diversion...take away our attention from something or maybe someone else.

-Like what or who? And, a chill just went up my back.

-Maybe, Correa's being manipulated.

-By?

-A sleazy funeral parlor director who I wouldn't trust from here to where your sitting. Don't look at me like that Lieutenant. All this is guess work and, again, pretty circumstantial. Was any evidence found at the crimes scenes?

-Fingerprints.

-You're kidding? Was there any match up?

-No. As a matter of fact, running them through F.B.I. files was a waste of time. They laughed at us; but, we weren't laughing.

-I don't get you.

The Lieutenant shifted in his chair. He put the sheet of paper back in its file, took out a cigarette and lit up.

-The fingerprints we found weren't made by a human being.

-What? Then, what in God's name made them?

-The fingerprints were an exact match at each crime scene, too. So, Mendez, we're looking for a serial killer who isn't human or animal. That's why I thought of you.

-Then, what is he? You got any idea?

-The autopsy reports kind of stumped the coroner: each victim had been dead for months.

-But, that can't be. Maybe our killer is spreading some kind of disease.

Lt. Donovan almost laughed.

-Now, you sound like me; but, I've been warned by my superiors not to even *think* such thoughts. They don't want a panic on our hands. I'm told that the coroners are taking every precaution with the bodies; none of which have been released to the nearest of kin.

The Lieutenant paused to take a sip of water.

-And, we know for a fact that four of the victims were alive and healthy on the day they were killed. How this maniac does it...I'm asking you that question, Mendez.

-Beats the hell out of me. But, my old friend, Marlena Lake...this is right up her alley.

\*\*\*

It was nearly evening when Nathalie Montaigne packed her two suitcases and was ready to leave the Waldorf Astoria Hotel. She looked out the window on to Park Avenue. It was cloudy and cold outside with more snow on the way according to the weather forecast.

The Frenchwoman had entertained the thought of simply walking out without bothering to pay her bill...her money had just about run out. But, her good friend and benefactor, Werner Hoffman, had come to her rescue. He would pay the hotel bill in full and help his French friend to find other lodgings.

-Nathalie? I've paid for you to stay two more days. But, we must find an apartment for you and there is also other business to attend to.

-There is much to do, Werner. But, where does one start? And, are you up to it, my dear?

-I'm fine. I've recovered my senses or what was left of them. My attempted suicide was a foolish act. I have a new desire to live and settle accounts.

Nathalie was sitting in front of a vanity mirror putting the finishing touches on her make-up. Her gray hair had been cut short and the make-up that she was applying was minimal.

-You look good, my dear. A little older, but still attractive.

-Not beautiful, eh? That prize, I could never claim. Come, Werner, we have a visit to make and it can no longer be put off. Are the police still following you, cherie? They've no cause to.

-They gave up on me right after the sun made its reappearance. What could I tell them about my former Nazi comrades? Nothing that they don't already know.

Nathalie gathered up her purse and gloves.

-But, that is not entirely true.

-I know nothing of immediate import.

-That's a much better way of phrasing it.

-And, what about yourself? There was no warrant for your arrest?

-None that I know of. And, what did I do? What crime did I commit, eh? Attempted robbery in a mausoleum? The police have far better things to occupy their time. There's a serial killer on the loose, no?

-I've read about it. But, still, it's best to keep a low profile.

-You've always been cautious. Shall we go?

Their destination was the Burn Unit at Roosevelt Hospital. They were going to visit Catrina Mendez. The reason for this unlikely visit: Miss Mendez had survived her journey through the black tunnel of transportation that the Nazis in Antarctica had used.

Nathalie Montaigne and Werner Hoffman stood outside Catrina Mendez's hospital door. They wanted to make certain that there was no one in the room with her: bumping into old "friends" was not on their agenda and it could prove more than just embarrassing. Not a sound could be heard coming from the patient's room, so the two people went in.

Nathalie touched her friend's elbow and whispered.

-Werner, over there behind the curtain.

They walked around the movable barrier to face Catrina Mendez lying in bed. She was propped up and her entire body was covered in gauze bandages with the exception of her hands and face which were scarred.

Nathalie again whispered to her companion.

-Is she awake. I don't see any movement.

The body on the bed spoke.

-I am quite awake. Who are you and what are you doing in my room?

The two visitors were taken aback by the harshness and, yes, cruelty of that voice. Werner Hoffman addressed the patient.

-My name is Werner Hoffman, Miss Mendez. And, this is my close associate, Nathalie Montaigne. Do you recognize those two names?

Catrina's eyes shifted from one to the other of her two visitors.

-Yes. You were associates of my father. What do you want with me?

-You come straight to the point, Miss Mendez.

-You have not answered my question.

Nathalie spoke up, but couldn't help stare at the scarred hands and face. She had seen such injuries before, but where?

-Miss Mendez, I was at the séance which your brother, Edward, conducted just a few weeks ago to summon your father.

-I remember it. It was I who warned you against it.

-The sacred object was found and used quite successfully. But, surely, you're aware of this.

Catrina laughed, if one could call it a laugh.

-I know. How very lucky you all were that the spear didn't kill you. My brother, Edward, is more adept than I thought.

-What do you mean by that?

Nathalie was close to anger. Even in pain, the bed-ridden woman was arrogant.

-My brother wielded its power? That was a question.

-Yes. Of course. But, my dear, we have not come about that.

-Haven't you?

-No. We want to ask you a question.

-Is that all? Why do you keep staring at my hands?

-Your injuries are familiar to me. Forgive me for staring.

-What is your question?

-Werner, perhaps you had better ask it.

-No. You ask it.

-It concerns your mother, Miss Mendez, and to an extent even yourself. Why has Mrs. Mendez isolated herself ever since your father's death? It's more than curiosity that makes me ask.

-Why not ask her?

Werner Hoffman was getting impatient with a woman he felt no sympathy for.

-We are asking *you*. And, if we must, we'll ask her.

-Fear. One day, a self-appointed Anti-Christ will attempt to raise the dead.

The two visitors took in this information.

-Who is this Anti-Christ?

-I don't know. But, he is someone familiar with death. My father may have known him. He knew many dangerous people and brought them to our house.

-Manuel Mendez knew this man? Raise the dead? For what purpose?

-Does a megalomaniac need a purpose?

-You're smarter than one would suspect, Miss Mendez. When is this to happen? Who is about to sound Gabriel's horn?

-Every day, my mother and I dreaded the event…his appearance. At first, I refused to believe it.

-But, now you're not so sure, eh?

-They bring me the papers. That serial killer…his victims…there may be a connection. I don't know. Please, leave me. I'm very tired.

-Of course. But, one more question, if I may? Will you return to your home in Brooklyn?

-I've nowhere else to go.

-We'll take our leave. Good day.

Outside in the hallway.

-Well, my dear Nathalie, what did you make of that?

-I'm surprised that she was so forthcoming.

-Yes. I hadn't expected that either. And she certainly knows a great deal about the occult. Did you notice how familiar she was with the Spear of Longinus? I found that most interesting.

-Indeed. Miss Catrina Mendez has been well trained. That veneer of shallowness that she presented to the world was a disguise.

-And, to raise the dead? How? To what end?

-To kill the living?

-Maybe. But, I'm not so sure that we can trust the woman.

-Werner, did you notice those scars on her hands and face?

-You couldn't miss them.

-It may be a coincidence, but I saw a dead man with similar scars. He had some kind of accident with the train.

-So? People are injured every day. You think there's some kind of a connection?

-You never know.

-Let's head for the elevator.

-It bothered me at the time.

-Why?

-I'm not certain, but-

-Go on. Here's the elevator. Let's get in. That nurse over there is staring at us.

-I'd like to find out who that man was. I need to put my curiosity to rest. But, how would we go about doing it? We can't go to the authorities.

-No. But, we might go to Mr. Edward Mendez. At least, I can. But, it will have to wait. We have to find you a permanent hiding place.

# Chapter Six
# January 8, 1948

-THERE'S SOMETHING I gotta' do tonight. I've been hiding out long enough, but now I've gotta' move.

-You can't go out into the street. You'll be spotted. Two days isn't nearly enough time to wait. You're too impulsive.

-Maybe. But, that's a chance I've gotta' take. I need me another male victim.

-Another one? That could be very dangerous. Haven't you killed enough lately?

-I've got my "orders."

-Who's ordering you?

-You'll find out one day if you're a good girl.

-Where will you find this victim? No. I don't want to know.

-You're starting to disappoint me, Anna. Better be careful.

-You'd better wait until the night comes if you're going out. I think it might snow again.

-I've gotta' meet someone before then. I'd better leave now. It's almost dark anyway.

He put his bomber jacket on.

-After I leave, turn your radio on and listen for the latest news bulletins. You might see the flames from here. Yeah. You just might get an eyeful.

Anna locked the door after he left and turned on the radio.


The news bulletin came at 10 P.M. that evening. Anna was taking inventory. She made herself a cup of American tea and it was lying on the wooden counter next to the cash register. She would have thrown the foul tasting liquid down the drain, but she didn't believe in waste. She had relatives to bring over from China and she needed every dollar that she could earn from her strict economizing and from the income brought through her merchandising. She stopped taking inventory for a moment and picked up the cup of neglected tea. She sipped the tea and made a face.

-Awful. Tastes like rust.

Anna had neither milk nor sugar to dilute the bitter taste because she was on a strict budget and diet. She needed to be at her most attractive to entice male customers. She put the half finished cup of tea back on  the counter.

-I'm tired and bored; but, I must finish this inventory. It's a shame that I can't hire any help.

And, then, the news bulletin came over the radio.


"The top news story of the day occurred a few minutes ago in lower Manhattan. Sullivan's Gymnasium went up in flames. Local residents thought they heard an explosion prior to the building catching fire, but these reports are unconfirmed.

"The fire is still raging as firefighters and police have converged on the scene. So far, no casualties have been reported as the gym was closed for the day. The gym's manager, Randy Bates, is on the scene , but has not been available for comment. Firefighters fear the blaze may spread to adjoining buildings. One eye witness thought he saw two men leaving the building just prior to the reported explosion, but that has not been confirmed either."

Anna turned the radio off.

-What have you done, Angel? And, who was that with you? Are you trying to get caught?

***

-Well, Mr. Angel Ulysses Correa, how does it feel to be a dead man? Not so traumatic for an immortal like yourself, eh?

Mr. Turhan Aswan locked the front door to his funeral parlor.

-It's still not official, pal. They gotta' find the body we left behind and make the connection to yours truly.

-Not "the body" - your "body." And, they'll find it all right – right where we left it. The police and the insurance people are quite thorough. I speak from experience. Let's go downstairs and talk. We don't want to attract attention up here.

Angel followed the funeral director down the narrow staircase and into the main waiting area. His shoes were wet from the slush in the streets.

-Sit down, my friend and let's talk about our next move.

-I guess I'll be leaving the country.

-Not just yet. You'll stay here until the current news dies down and you're put to rest.

-I've got a hiding place with this Asian chick.

-Does she know about you?

-She's up on her occult stuff, if that's what you mean.

Angel laughed and took off his jacket.

-And, would you believe it? She wants what I've got.

-Interesting girl that you found. I'd like to meet her. But, in the meantime, you stay here. I'll put you up in the sub-basement. We'll look after you.

-No. You're not keeping me locked up like some kind of animal. You want me to leave the damned country? Fine. I'll head to South America.

-Not as far as that, surely.

-Why not? I speak the lingo. But, I've gotta' couple of scores to settle first.

-Tell me who you want to kill.

-That bitch, Valerie, who got me into this.

Turhan Aswan leaned forward, almost touching Angel's outstretched legs.

-You should be grateful to that "bitch." In a way, you owe her your immortality. Without her, you'd be a poor, young man hustling out an existence as an amateur bodybuilder. Your prospects would be limited by blind luck and the passage of time. You'd end your life in the slums where we found you. But, if you want to kill her, I can't stop you.

-Don't even try.

-Don't threaten me. I am what you are and with years of killer experience. You think you can survive on your own? Forget it. I warned you once before not to take my generosity for granted.

Angel smiled.

-Wouldn't dream of it, man. And, just maybe you talked me into postponing Valerie's death scene.

-You've been a little too careless and wild, but that was to be expected with the first flush of immortal vigor.

Angel kicked off his shoes.

-Got a cigarette?

-I'm all out. I'll have Aniika pick me up a carton tomorrow. You all out?

-Must've dropped my pack in all the excitement tonight.

-You said you had a "couple" of scores to settle. Who else do you mean to kill?

-You don't know him; but, I do.

-Why not wait until the next new moon when you will actually need to kill?

-'Cause I don't feel like it.

-Who is the intended victim?

-Edward Mendez.

-I've met him. He's a private investigator. You might have trouble there. I'd advise against it.

-Why? Not that I'll listen.

-You had better listen. Mr. Mendez has direct contacts with the police. And, I don't just mean your typical patrol officer. He knows people in high places. Keep away from him, at least for now. Savvy? That's not a request, Angel. You'll place us all in danger with your arrogance and cavalier attitude.

-I get the message. He's got this girlfriend, I think.

-Stay away from her, as well.

-She's an ice skater.

-Did you hear what I just said? Stay away from her.

-I'll talk with the chick, that's all.

-No, you fool. Don't get Mendez angry.

-Why the fuck not? I won't hurt her too much. I might even be nice.

-You don't listen, do you? Mendez also has other contacts that are of interest to me. I don't want them jeopardized.

-Like what?

Aswan didn't want to tell him. The less he knew about the organization's long term plans, the better for everyone. This boy was too wild. He had to be tamed and maybe even taught a hard lesson. Tonight, Angel had severed ties with his past more than the young boy could imagine.

***

Yolanda was practicing her straight line sequence. It was getting close to midnight; but, she wasn't about to let that stop her. Her linear movement was steady if just a little too slow. She knew that she had to improve it or she would never make it to the medal podium.

-I have to stop being afraid of making a mistake.

She tried again, but this time faster. Not too bad.

-If I can just get by these "figures," I should be okay. I've got the double axel and the double salchow down cold. My technical scores should hold up.

Yolanda adjusted her hair ribbon and pulled at her sweat shirt. A few spectators were sitting in the upper benches watching her. She waved to them and they waved back and cheered. Her coach was due back any minute and the figure skater wanted his input on the quality of her "figures."

She took a handkerchief out of her skirt pocket and dabbed at her forehead. A man standing on the edge of the rink caught her attention. He was gesturing for Yolanda to come over to him. She waved to the man and skated a few feet closer to the edge of the ice rink and stopped. He was a stranger and Yolanda didn't trust strangers.

The young man shouted over to her.

-Come here. I want to talk to you about someone.

The young man was choosing his words with care. He was trying to hide the hardness and coarse tone of his voice. Yolanda wasn't taken in.

He spoke, again, and this time the hardness of his nature broke through.

-Don't make me shout. And, don't make me come over to you.

-What do you want?

-I want to talk to your lousy boyfriend.

-Who are you?

-He'll know who I am, lady. And, I said move closer.

-You can go to the devil. I'll bet you don't even know who my boyfriend is.

-You'd lose. He's Edward Mendez, P. I.

Yolanda wasn't sure how she ought to respond. The young man smiled at her and put one foot on to the ice.

-Keep away. I'll scream.

-Won't do you any good.

He was now standing on the ice.

Yolanda moved back and was about to scream for help to the spectators she had waved to before. But, the young man fell face forward on to the ice.

-Not so easy to walk on ice, is it?

He got to his knees and was about to speak, but choked on his words.

Yolanda took the opportunity to skate over to the opposite end of the rink. The young man hugged his arms about his torso. Now, he spoke.

-The cold...the cold is killing me, you bitch! You lousy, stinking bitch! My body...it's freezing. Fuck!

He struggled to get off the ice and back on to solid ground. It took a few seconds for him to recover enough of his strength to gain control of his faculties. He turned around and shouted across the ice at Yolanda.

-Tell your private dick that I'll get him and you. You tell him that Angel's on his tail. He won't be safe 'till I'm six feet under. You got that?

Yolanda knew enough not to answer. She watched as Angel walked out of the building, still hugging his arms about his torso. He glanced back at her and walked out the door.

Yolanda waited a few minutes and, then, rushed over to one of the pay phones by the restrooms. Her coach was just coming out.

Angel had disobeyed Turhan's orders to stay hidden. He found that one of the debased joys in being an immortal was putting fear into his victims; didn't much matter if it was short or long term. Fear did something to the victim's blood: it raised the temperature of the fluid and the bleeding was quicker. He knew that the figure skater would be practicing late so he had made his move to terrify her and that would trigger the P. I.'s manhunt. Angel would be ready for him.

It was now well past midnight as Angel Correa walked down 8th Avenue toward the West Village. Aswan would be angry with him, but not surprised. The undertaker knew that he was a wild card and that the youth needed a long leash.

It was a cold January night, but there was no wind so Angel found the weather almost tolerable. He'd have preferred a much warmer climate, but for the moment, he was stuck in New York City.

He was a loner walking the streets and he felt the loss of contact with his parents and best friend, Jaime. He and his gym buddy had shared so much. Their friendship had endured despite Angel's moods and Jaime's homosexuality. Why should Angel care that his friend preferred male lovers? He didn't judge Jaime and in a way he was sorry that the couldn't respond to Jaime's advances...and there had been a few veiled ones as well as the steam room incident..

And, Angel had no idea that his best friend was dead because he didn't kill him; that had been the work of another immortal.

Anna opened the door to let Angel inside.

-Do you know what time it is?

-No.

-It doesn't matter to you, I know.

-Keep the lights off. I need to talk to you. I want to talk before you become too involved. There's still time to pull out. I'm giving you that chance.

Anna led the way to the back room.

-Here. Sit down.

She gestured to a wooden folding chair. Angel sat down and stretched his legs. He still had on his bomber jacket. Anna sat on the edge of her twin bed.

-So what do you want to talk to me about? I'm tired and I have to open shop tomorrow morning...actually, it's already tomorrow morning.

-I've gotta' tell someone how it all started. You want to know. I know you do.

Anna was wide awake now. She buttoned up her housecoat. It was chilly in the small room.

-Yes, Angel! I don't deny it. Tell me everything.

It was the first time she'd spoken his name. Angel took out a pack of cigarettes and slipped one out.

-I don't read the papers, so I don't know too much about what's going on in the world. I follow people instead. I hunt 'em down and move in for the kill. I'm not supposed to do that. It's suppose to happen at the new moon each month.

He extended his pack of cigarettes to Anna.

-Smoke? It'll help keep you awake.

-No. Angel, start at the very beginning and take your time. Try not to leave anything out.

Angel lit his cigarette and took a deep drag.

-Okay, babe, here's my story. Better listen.

# Part Two
## Angel Ulysses Correa

# Chapter One
# December 13, 1947

-I'M A young man, Anna, who's being eaten alive with hatred. This hatred and bitterness, man, takes up every damned part of me. At times, it kind of fades beneath the surface when I'm at the gym and working out, but that's about the only time. And, it's real funny because that's where it all started: at the gymnasium on that cold December day.

***

I was working out with my friend, Jaime Morillo. We were just finishing up our free-weight program. It was a late afternoon on a Friday in the early part of December.

Too bad the sun had gone from the sky. We opened up the window, but it was too damned cold out so we had to close it real fast.

I put the barbell back into its slot, wiped my forehead and then we headed downstairs to the locker room on the main floor. Jaime was right on my tail. We stripped down and headed downstairs to the shower area. The floor felt kind of cold on our bare feet, but we got used to it. We were naked, but there was no one around so it didn't matter...not that it would anyway. We didn't mind showing off our hard, sculpted bodies. We worked hard enough for them.

We turned on the shower taps and started lathering up. Jaime was scrutinizing my body and there was no big deal in that.

-Gave you a good shave the other day. You still look smooth.

He touched my chest with his forefinger.

-Just a little bit of a razor burn, but not much. You do good work, Mr. Morillo. Maybe, you oughta' be a barber. Got any plans for the weekend?

-No.

-Me neither; but, I practically never do. Who's your friend over there?

-Got me, man. Never saw him before. I think he's trying to pick up a pretty boy.

Jaime let out a laugh and flung some water in my face.

-Maybe. And, maybe, he wants a fist down his throat.

I said this loud enough so that he'd be sure to hear it. The stranger backed away and headed up the stairs. I turned back to Jaime who was staring at the retreating figure.

-What's up?

-Angel, did you see that guy's face?

-No.

-It was fucking awful, man. Old...and with a million lines all over it...or scars.

Jaime turned about and washed his face, shaking his body clean of something that gave him the willies. I put my hand on his back.

-You feeling better?

He turned to me and tried to smile.

-A little.

He patted me on the cheek.

-Let's go into the steam room, Angel, and talk.

-Okay. But, we don't have much time. The evening rush is coming in pretty soon and I don't want to be here.

-Just a few minutes. Do you mind?

-Let's go. I'm finished here anyway.

We turned off the shower and walked over to the steam room. Just before we went in, I happened to look up to the top of the staircase and saw that stranger standing there.

-What's he up to?

-Never mind him, let's steam off.

We got into the steam room and slammed the glass door behind us. We dropped our towels to the floor. Jaime put his arms around me.

-You feel good, Angel: hard and tight.

-What's wrong? Tell me.

I felt real awkward by then. I didn't know what to do or how to react. I was surprised, but not repulsed. And, then, Jaime kissed me on the mouth: hard and wet. I pushed him away. Now, it was Jaime who felt awkward and even ashamed of himself. He was also trying to hide his erection.

-I'm sorry, Angel.

I wiped my mouth and asked him again.

-What's wrong? Tell me.

-It's that guy.

-What's your problem with him? And, if he's still out there, I'm gonna' use him for a punching bag. Now, what's up?

-I don't know. I just don't know.

Jaime sat down on the tile ledge and put his face in his hands.

-Angel, what I just did-

-It never happened.

-But, I've been wanting-

-It never happened.

-Okay.

-Let's get out of here. It's too hot and we both need to get home. You coming?

-Not yet. I'll see you tomorrow at the photo session.

-I don't like leaving you like this.

-Don't worry about me.

-I do worry. Let me worry. You take care of yourself and be on time tomorrow.

I left the steam room in a hurry, rinsed myself off in the shower and climbed the stairs to get back to the locker room. I got dressed and zipped up my canvas gym bag, a present from my dad, and walked over to the sink to check out how I looked. Not bad. I ran a comb through my short, black hair and put my wire rimmed glasses back on. It was time to leave.

In another couple of seconds, I was back on the street and headed for the subway. The day was pretty much done for and I felt like I didn't have a care in the world. But, just maybe that wasn't really true. I slung my duffel bag over my shoulder and climbed down the subway stairs. It was pretty dark and there was only one over-head light bulb working in the narrow corridor that led to the token booth. When I reached the bottom of the stairs, I found myself standing right in front of that man who'd been at the gym.

-What's your problem?

-I beg your pardon?

-You following me or something? You're blocking my way.

It was too dark to get a good look at his face.

-I have a great problem, as you phrase it.

-Let me see who I'm talking to.

-That would not be advisable, young man. My face is an abhorrence even to myself. It would not please you at all to see it, as I so carelessly allowed your friend to.

-Jaime?

-Is your friend Spanish? I thought that one could detect the Castilian blood in him. The two of you are fine specimens. But, you are aware of your beauty.

-What of it?

-It was not an accusation.

-What do you want?

-A short and direct question.

-How many times am I gonna' have to ask it?

-I want to warn you of a visit that I will one day make to your home, Angel Correa.

-How do you know my name?

-The young man behind the desk at your gymnasium informed me. The transaction cost me five dollars.

-Must've been Randy. He'll do anything for a buck. So, who are you?

-Someone who needs to make your acquaintance before it's too late. I must go now; but, let me tell you this, young man.

-I'm listening.

-Pay careful attention to new acquaintances.

-What is that suppose to mean?

-Don't make any new friends no matter how "nice" or persuasive they may seem. I must leave you now.

He brushed past me and ran up the stairs, leaving me just standing there.

In about another hour, the train pulled into my stop in Brooklyn and I had to practically shove my way out on to the platform. The doors slid closed behind me. I just made it on to the platform.

I debated whether or not to stop in at the candy store that was underneath the station. I needed some chewing gum so I went inside to buy a pack. I bought two packs because I chew on a lot of gum: a habit that drives Jaime to distraction. Too bad for Mr. Jaime Miguel Morillo: a real Latin charmer when he put his mind to it. No girlfriends, though, and maybe today I found out the reason why. Anyway, I paid for my gum, unwrapped one of the silver wrappers and stuck two pieces of the sweet stuff into my mouth.

When I reached my corner, the sidewalks were pretty empty. It was nearly supper time and families were getting ready to eat. I made my way down the block and to my apartment building...and I saw my mother waiting for me on our stoop.

-Angel, thank God you're home. And, it's about time, young man.

-Why? What's up?

-Come inside. I don't want to talk out here in the open. It's too frightening with no sun in the sky.

Up until then, I tried putting the missing sun out of my mind.

We walked into the small vestibule and away from public sight.

-Let's go upstairs. I've gotta' put a coat on and get my bag.

-Like, what's wrong?

She put on her coat and reached for her black bag that was crammed with papers, money, keys, pencils, and God knew what else.

-Now, we can go.

-Go where, for Christ's sake? You haven't told me anything.

-Let's go outside and wait for the cab.

She practically ran out of the apartment, leaving me to lock up. I didn't even have time to take a leak.

-We're taking a cab? Since when? To go where?

-To the hospital. Your father's been hurt.

-What happened? An accident on the job?

-A crane snapped in half and smashed into a wall and some of the debris hit your father. I didn't want to leave until you got home. Oh, there's the cab.

She waved her arms and shouted at the top of her lungs.

By the time we arrived at the hospital, my dad had been moved from the Emergency Room to a regular bed. We were told to wait in the reception area and it felt like we were waiting there for a real long time.

I excused myself to go the the bathroom. And, for a hospital toilet, it was pretty filthy. I went over to the urinal to relieve myself. Out of the corner of my eye, I saw that strange man who I'd run into in the subway tunnel. I was still holding my rod in my hand, trying to get a good look at this guy. I couldn't make out his face because of his wide brimmed hat being pulled down. I stuffed my rod back into my trousers and walked over to the sink to wash up.

The door opened up behind me and a cop walked in. We nodded to each other as I turned to leave.

My mother was still in the waiting room when I got back.

-Still no word?

-I'm sick of waiting here. Who the hell do they think they are keeping us in the dark like this? I'm his wife.

-What time is it?

-There's a clock over there: just past 8:30.

-Let's just go on up. Like, who's gonna' stop us?

-You're right. It's room 403. I asked one of the nurses when we came in.

We took the elevator up to the fourth floor. My father's room was the first door to the right. I rapped on the door, opened it and stuck my head in.

-Dad?

-Come on in, Angel. And, Louisa...I wasn't expecting anyone.

My mom went over to my dad and started asking a lot of questions. He looked good and I really couldn't tell what if anything was wrong with him.

There was another patient in the room and he had a visitor. I could just make her out behind the curtain that separated the two beds. She got up and introduced herself.

-My name's Valerie Vandor. What's yours?

-Angel Correa.

I liked what I saw. She was young and had a pretty good figure. She had short, red hair that I think was bleached. Her face was a little on the weak side but her eyes were striking and heavily made up.

I gestured toward the man in the bed.

-Is your friend behind the curtain all right? He doesn't look too good.

-He might live. As a matter if fact, he probably will; but, forget about him. He's fast asleep, anyway.

Her manner was real off-handed. I noticed that she was wearing a sports blazer and pants and black, stiletto heels. The look suited her to a "T."

-What's wrong with the guy? Is he your father, Angel? You look like him.

-He's my dad, all right.

-Is she your mother? She looks more like your grandmother.

I laughed.

-Don't tell her that.

-So, what happened to him?

She kept flinging her head back in this real affected manner, all the while looking me straight in the eye and expecting immediate answers.

-Work accident. He's a bricklayer and he got hurt, but not too bad.

-Why don't you get him checked out of this dump?

-Now?

-Why not? Who's to stop you? He looks fine to me.

-I don't know. Aren't there release forms or something you've gotta' sign?

-Let your mother take care of that. Come on. Introduce me.

That chick just took over. She convinced my father to check himself out which wasn't so hard because he hated hospitals. My mother didn't mind so much either; but, I don't think she liked Valerie.

The two of us stepped out into the hallway while my mother helped my dad to get ready.

-Okay, handsome, where do we go from here?

-Go where?

-We can put your parents in a cab and, then, go and have a bite to eat. You got any money on you?

-Not much. I never eat out. Maybe, I should just go on home. It's been a long day.

-With Mommy and Daddy? No. I don't think you oughta' do that. Come with me and we'll go to this all night dive that's only a couple of blocks from here. We can have some coffee and hamburgers. I've got a couple of bucks on me. I'll cover you.

-I can't just leave.

-Why not, Angel? Your parents will know you went off with a pretty girl and they'll respect you for it. Well...at least your dad will. Your mother will probably hate me. Tough. Let's go.

Before I knew it, the two of us were sitting down in this eatery that was "shoveled in" under the elevated train with a lot of cheap bargain stores. It was a part of town that was only two train stops from my own neighborhood.

-Hey, Valerie, look at the time. I didn't think it was so damned late.

-Past eleven o'clock. I like that. Means we've got the whole night ahead of us and time passes a lot slower at night than it does during the day time even if the friggin' sun isn't there anymore. So, let's chat, handsome. Tell me all about yourself.

-There's not an awful lot to tell.

-Quit feeling sorry for yourself.

-It's kinda cramped in here and stuffy.

-Angel, talk to me.

-I'm nineteen and live at home. I had to drop out of high school and go to work. I didn't mind so much because I hated school. My dad's between jobs a lot and that meant no money coming in. And, it's not so easy finding work in construction; but, I hear that's about to change.

-What do you do for a living?

She was all smiles with that question because she probably couldn't see me doing anything much.

-When I can get jobs, I'm an artist's model. I also pose for magazine layouts. And, when I'm really desperate, I do janitor work around the gym which pays next to nothing.

-Nice! You've got the body for it. How'd you get into that line?

-I've always been interested in bodybuilding and health in general. It just seemed like a good thing to do for myself.

-I like it. But, you've gotta' stretch your salary between jobs just like your dad and that's tough.

-And, I've got expenses. The gymnasium costs money and I've gotta' take care of my skin and general appearance. I've got a job lined up today with my workout buddy, Jaime.

-Nice! Can I come along?

-I don't think so. They're mostly beefcake shots, you know. We'll be in posing straps and not much else.

-Oh God! That sounds wild! You're taking me.

-I-

-Listen, Angel, let me tell you a little bit about myself.

I went back to eating my hamburger; but, I listened.

-I'm a little older than you are. I'm twenty-one and we actually live only a few blocks from each other, but that's not important. But, this is and I want you to listen.

-Do you mind if I eat while I listen? I'm real hungry.

-Go ahead. You're young and beautiful and poor and do you know what that means? It means you're a loser because being poor is a crippling disease. It will kill everything else that you have going for you.

I nodded. I understood what she was telling me or at least I thought I did.

-What you need, Angel, is an unshakable confidence in yourself. You need to be willing to take risks...big risks. And, you've got to learn to look after yourself.

-Hey, Valerie, where you going with this lecture? It sounds real good, but it's only talk.

She leaned closer so that no one could overhear us.

-I belong to a group of very talented and interesting people. We're looking for a new member to replace an old one. It's an unusual sort of group. I want you to come with me tomorrow. I'll meet you after your modeling job – the one that I know you don't want to take me to – and we can go together. Say you'll come with me.

-I don't know. I usually go with Jaime and spend the evening with him and sometimes his sister, Consuelo.

-Doing what? Playing the radio and staring at each other or maybe more?

-I don't think I like what you just said. Watch your mouth.

-Down, boy. Val was just teasing.

-I don't like being teased.

-Sensitive type. That's good. Means that you're self-ish...and so am I. I can cope with a sensitive man. So, come with me.

-For what?

-To be a winner. Angel, we do ritual work.

-What's that?

-Magic. And, I mean real magic; not the crap that your local huckster does.

-You're over my head, now.

-We're doing a prosperity ritual tomorrow: a sort of laboratory experiment that just might generate wealth.

-Will it do any good?

-It depends on what you put into it. You have to give it everything that you can. You've got to be serious about it.

-I'm a pretty serious guy. And, why me? And, who was your friend  back at the hospital?

Valerie leaned back in her chair and appraised me with a new sort of respect.  She lit herself a cigarette.

-You're sharper than I thought. I like you and your gorgeous body. Honest enough for you?

-Keep it going.

-That was my less than useless father in the hospital bed.

-What the hell happened to him?

-He was in an accident of sorts. I might as well tell you. He tried killing himself and it's not the first time, either. He's lucky that he's still breathing. But, forget about him because you can't do anything for him. He can't even help himself. So, what's your answer?

-I'll go with you. What have I got to lose? Where are *we* going anyway?

-Now, don't be put off. It's in a funeral parlor.

-You're kidding me?

-I know! It is pretty weird; but, it's the appropriate place.

I gulped down the last of the lousy coffee while Valerie gave the place the once over.

-Look around you, Angel, and what do you see? What I see is dirt and poverty and that poor woman over there by the counter eating some day old hash and not wanting to leave because she's so lonely and miserable. What we do is dangerous, but what of it? What's the alternative? We do things that people don't approve of. We play with death and life.

Valerie looked at me with her alluring but hard eyes.

-Do you want to play with us?

-I don't mind playing too much, but toward what end?

She reached across the table and touched my hand.

-What you just asked me is the most wonderful thing you could have said. You're already one of us. I *knew* I would meet you tonight.

-Who else is in your group?

-You'll meet them all tomorrow. It's a fairly small group. There's a Mr. Juan Ortega who does most of Turhan's dirty work. Then, there's the practical Diane from the U. K. She's got a weight problem but it's not too bad, really. Who else?

She took a sip of her coffee and continued

-There's Mohamed, who's sort of second-in-command, but he's really just a glorified messenger boy. Oh, yes, there's Aniika who's Turhan's wife. And, she's in it over her pretty little head. So, Angel, where will I meet you?

-Twenty-third and Sixth Ave. at about five o'clock. That okay?

-It'll have to be. Do you have a suit that you can wear?

-I'm not wearing it. I told you: I've got a photo session and I don't want to carry anything more than I have to.

-Like a posing strap is a lot to carry?

-There's more to it than that. You wouldn't understand.

-Let's get out of here. I'll get the check.

# Chapter Two
## December 14, 1947

THE NEXT day, when I stepped out of the subway and was headed for the gym, the air felt heavy, but there was no sign of rain. But, with all the darkness in the sky, who could tell?. I went into the gym and saw that Jaime had signed in. I did likewise. When I turned around, I almost collided with Jaime's sister, Consuelo.

-Hey, Consuelo, good to see you.

She smiled warmly and not only with the curves of her lips but with her eyes.

-I've been well. And, how are you and your parents?

I told her about my dad and she asked me to send him her best wishes.

-May we speak for a minute? I won't keep you. I know that you're anxious to train with Jaime.

Yesterday's incident in the steam room flashed through my mind.

-Jaime was very agitated when he came home yesterday. I couldn't get him to confide in me. And, it was the same this morning. You're his best friend, Angel. Do you know what's wrong? I've never seen him like this.

-There was a strange man here yesterday. Jaime caught a glimpse of his face and it scared him real bad.

-Did you also see this man's face? Was it so terrible?

I didn't get a chance to answer because Jaime came down the stairs.

-You're gonna' get soft just standing there, Angel.

Consuelo smiled at her brother.

-It's all my fault.

I spoke to Consuelo.

-Are you staying? We're gonna' be a while.

-I have some shopping to do; but, I'll wish you both good luck with your photo session. I'll even buy a copy when the magazine comes out. And, you both better autograph it for me.

My workout with Jaime went well. We spotted each other on the weights and encouraged and pushed one another to try even harder. The two hours went by real fast and by that time, we were soaking in sweat. We hit the showers and, then, hurried upstairs to get dressed.

***

The photo session was done in the barest of settings with props at a minimum. The lighting was done with just one of those klieg lights that they use in the movies. The camera was on a tripod. And, we seldom used our posing straps. We posed in the raw, but the camera man told us the photos would be in good taste with no frontal nudity.

A few shots were taken of the two of us together on a Greek pedestal. The camera man took his time with this particular shot because it was supposed to make the cover of the magazine. The pedestal scraped against our bare butts and at one point, we almost lost our balance and slipped off the base.

At last, the session was over and Jaime almost ran to get his clothes back on. He was trying to hide a semi-erection which can be embarrassing. It happened to me a couple of times. The size of a man's dick wasn't something talked about or paraded around with for effect.

Jaime left without me, because I'm a slow dresser and he was in a hurry to get home. I didn't mind because Valerie would be downstairs waiting for me.

\*\*\*

Valerie was waiting on the corner and not looking too pleased. She was wearing this real nice black dress.

-Glad you came, Angel. How'd the photo shoot go?

-I guess it went okay.

-Let's go. They're waiting for us.

-I should warn you that I'm kind of shy around people. I'm not so good at small talk.

-That's okay. And, I forgive you for not wearing a suit like I asked you to. I just didn't want you to feel out of place.

I didn't want to go with Valerie and that hit me like a ton of bricks. I wanted to break away from her and hop on that downtown bus to be with Jaime and Consuelo. But, Valerie had me in her grasp; and, I just didn't have enough will power to pull away. And, before I knew it, we were standing in front of the funeral parlor.

-Let's go in. And, swallow that damned gum. It's really annoying.

I spit it out and we walked in.

-We're going into that closed room over to your right.

-Right about now, I'd give anything to be at home with the radio playing.

-Oh, God, Angel! You are a bore. Let's go in.

The first thing I noticed was the coffin: an open coffin with a cadaver in it.

-I'm getting' the hell out of here.

-Angel, just shut up.

Three dim lamps were giving off light: two of them were flanking the coffin and there was a tiny lamp set into a desk right above the "sign in" book where mourners gave money and recorded their names. There were five rows of folding chairs with the front row reserved for a sort of a sofa.

-Who's the stiff in the coffin?

-A victim.

-A what?

-Forget it.

I kept staring at the corpse...expecting it to come alive.

-Come on. Let's pay our last respects to the dear man. Then, I'll introduce you to everyone. And, don't be afraid because it won't be appreciated.

The corpse was the brightest thing in the room with the clean, white bandages reflecting the dim lights. We went up to the coffin.

-Say a prayer, Angel. Send the poor soul on its way.

-You've gotta' be kidding.

-Say it, aloud.

-Forget it. I don't pray.

-Just do it.

-I can't do it. I don't know how; this Catholic boy is out of practice.

-You can and you will.

I tried thinking of something...anything because I could feel all these people staring at my back. I folded my hands across my chest.

-Hear my prayer, gods of the great journey into the night. Bear the soul from this body toward heaven where time does not wield its terrible power. Let the infinite journey of this man begin...bear his soul into the night sky above and place him among the stars. Amen.

I uncrossed my arms.

-Oh, God, Angel! You were wonderful. I just knew you'd know what to do. Come on. I'll introduce you to the others.

We turned to face the others.

-Angel, this is Diane Price.

-Charmed. That was a rather lovely prayer. Welcome to our little group, luv.

Mr. Juan Ortega was next.

-Hello, Angel. May I call you by your first name? It's good that you came tonight. Your prayer was good...very good. We'll talk later, my friend.

-Angel, this is our leader, Mr. Turhan Aswan.

I was staring face to face with this bronze statue of a bastard. His eyes were dark and penetrating. His copper hair was a little too long and that pencil mustache made him look like one of those fops you hear about.

-We are pleased to welcome you to our fold. You're staring at my face.

-Didn't mean to stare. Sorry. I don't like it when people stare at me.

-I didn't take offense. You should stare. My tan is quite deep and how unfortunate that in a few days time it will all but fade. I will once again be my pale, Egyptian self. Now, please sit down next to me so that we may talk.

He turned to face his wife, Aniika, who was a petite woman and a little older than her husband.

-Aniika, dear, would you take the others downstairs so that I may speak to our young man in private?

-Of course. And, Angel, I bid you welcome. Try to ignore the surroundings.

She touched my hand with her fingertips. Did she want her husband to see that? The others followed her out and me and Aswan were left alone.

-Let's sit next to each other.

Just as we were about to sit down, the door opened and a man came rushing in.

-Forgive me, Turhan, for being so disgracefully late.

-Mohamed, we were wondering where you were. No harm done. This is Angel Correa.

-A pleasure, Mr. Correa. I'm glad you could come.

-If you'll excuse us, Angel and I must speak in private.

-Of course. Mr. Correa, you will excuse me?

He left the room almost as fast as when he came in. Again, we were alone. Aswan must have sensed my tenseness. I put my gym bag down between my legs.

-Angel, you must make your life's choice between the world that you know and my world of magic and infinite danger. I may tell you nothing more until you have made that decision.

-You don't waste any time. But, how the hell can I make that kind of a decision when I really don't know anything?

-Think back to the prayer that you uttered so masterfully just a few moments ago. Your instincts are razor sharp. You will be a valuable asset to us. Decide.

-If you're asking me to join then I guess my answer is "yes." Don't ask me why.

-Why?

-Don't like being poor. I'm- I'm untrained and uneducated. All I've got is this body of mine.

-It's good that you realize your present limitations. With out help, you will maintain your health and beauty.

He took out a cigarette.

-Would you mind if I smoke?

-Go ahead. My dad smokes all the time.

He inhaled on the cigarette and slowly let out a puff of smoke in my face.

-I needed that. Angel, have you ever wondered what lies beyond this life?

-No.

-You're young and healthy, so why should you?

I was getting a little tired of this roundabout talk that wasn't really telling my anything. On impulse, I got up to leave.

-Where are you going?

-I think I changed my mind. I don't do too well in groups. And, when I die...well, who knows? It's probably the end. So long, Mr. Aswan. Sorry I wasted-

Darkness. I felt the hard thump to the back of my head and, then, the crashing darkness.

\*\*\*

I woke up and found myself lying naked on a metal table.

-Are you awake, Angel?

I felt alert and kind of aware of myself in a real strange way that I can't explain. Even in my prone position on the cold table, I wasn't afraid. I was staring up at the ceiling that was painted black. It was like staring into outer space.

-What are you doing to me? Where the hell am I?

-We're changing your metabolism. Before this night is over, you'll be a creature of the sun and the flame. These elements will sustain your being and enhance your prowess. However, certain limitations will ensue. You'll have little tolerance for the cold and the evening hours will be a discomfit to you. Your sustenance will be that old cliché of other peoples' souls: their blood.

-Why are you doing this?

-To initiate you, of course. Oh, I have no illusions as to your loyalty for at the moment it's non-existent. You may leave us for a time; but, you'll be back.

-You're pretty sure of yourself, pal.

-The ritual is over and the bandages have been removed. We've even turned up the heat for you. We take care of our own. Now, get up and flex that chiseled body. You look a bit pale, but that will soon change.

Aswan helped me to get into a sitting position.

-Now, stand up straight. Look. Even your private member is stiff through the rush of blood.

He touched my rod.

-Don't do that, man.

-May I not?

-No. I don't like it.

-Too bad. We are brothers under the skin, as you would say. Let me help you with your clothes.

-My skin feels so damned dry. I feel like I"m about to drift out of my body.

-That will pass. All your clothes have been washed and made ready for you. You've been with us now for just over twenty-four hours.

-You're kidding me? I don't believe it.

-It's true. Now get dressed.

\*\*\*

-For some reason, Anna, that loss of a day put a real bad scare in me.

\*\*\*

Aswan walked over to the door and left. As the door clicked shut, my muscles and senses came back to life. I felt invigorated. In a couple of minutes, I was fully dressed and waiting for Aswan to come for me. There was a sharp knock on the door and it was "slid" open..

-Good. You're ready to come with me into the other room. Give me your hand and I'll lead you through the darkness.

Aswan brought me from the "operating" room and into the adjacent one which was the darkest room I had ever been in. There was no light at all. My eyes couldn't adjust because there were no points of reference. I got even more scared.

-We are, at this moment, Angel, in non-space and non-time. We're invisible to our enemies...and our enemies are our fellow members. They cannot see us or even intuit our presence. This room is a patch of utter blackness and nothingness that would frighten even the night sky of the heavens.

Aswan's words put a chill up my damned spine. In the next room, I could hear Valerie talking.

-Just remember, I've got dibs on him. I found him and he's mine. I've been scouting dear Angel for months. I know a prized specimen when I see one. Too bad Mohamed here hammered him one. But what's done cannot be undone. Isn't that what the old Bard would say?

The coldness in that bitch's voice made me want to rush in there and strangle her.

-Mohamed did the right thing. The boy was going to turn his back on us. And, what is there to argue about? The deed is accomplished.

I think that was Aswan's wife talking, Aniika.

-He's a fine specimen. I wonder if there's any Greek in him.

-Juan, you really are too obvious, luv.

-Do my musings offend you, Diane?

-Not at all. I was thinking along the same lines.

-It was I who struck the blow to the boy. I did what Turhan would have wanted: to give the boy no options. And after the incident with Henry Vandor, delay was no longer an option.

Aswan spoke to me.

-Angel? Time to go in. You can't see my eyes, but my cat's eyes can see yours. I'll have you driven home and I will go with you. Are you ready?

-I guess so.

-Say, yes.

-Yes.

-Come.

The other members greeted us and welcomed me as a new member. They tried not to stare, but they weren't too successful.

After a few minutes of strained conversation, Aswan, Valerie, and me said our goodbyes and headed for a limo that was parked outside. Valerie got into the driver's seat and me and Aswan slid into the back. The glass partition was up.

-Angel, when you sleep tonight, you may experience flashbacks of what was done to you. It might be disturbing, but don't try and resist the visions. When you awaken, you will be filled with vitality that may even be overwhelming. Conserve that energy and don't waste it on trifles. Do what you would normally do and try not to show off: save your energy for the night.

He leaned closer to me and this time I could see his dark eyes.

-You have changed and are no longer mortal. The urge will come upon you. Your victim's blood and tissue will provide you with the essence of fire and water that your body must have in order to regenerate itself. You must kill and kill effectively. I call it the kiss of the Phoenix. The victim is lured into your embrace. And, as you kiss them fully on the mouth, you plunge this into their solar plexus.

Aswan reached into his suit jacket and took out a small, gold dagger. At the tip of the dagger, was a tiny opening like the fang of a snake.

-This little surgical tool will ensure your victim's "pliability." I took the dagger and just stared at it.

-Put it in a safe place when you get the chance. And, by the way, at every new moon, you will need a victim. At other times, you can amuse yourself with the kill.

-Suppose I decide not to be a killer?

-You can choose to take your own life; that is an act of free will.

-I'm no killer.

-You will be. Don't underestimate yourself. Go into the city and visit the brothels of both sexes. Easy pickings! We may even run into each other some night.

-Why are we doing all this?

-To survive and even, maybe, to create a new race. It's been done before by the ancients. Now, sit back and relax.

The only light in the car was from the dashboard and the passing street lamps.

-We'll let you off on the corner. Don't want to arouse your neighbors' suspicions. And...yes. At the moment, there is no sun in the sky. But, the solar orb will return. I am confident.

Valerie double-parked the limo.

-Here we are. We'll keep in touch and there may be a few surprises for you. Take good care of yourself.

I got out of the car and slammed the door shut. I tapped on Valerie's window and waved goodbye. She waved back and drove off leaving me standing alone on my street corner.

When I got to my apartment building, I stopped to look up at the sky. The full moon was practically invisible because of the sun's disappearance, but the night stars in the sky glittered like diamonds. I could even see my favorite planet, Mars. I sat down on the front stoop and just brooded for a while. I was wide awake: what had I been turned into? A figure coming down the sidewalk caught my eye.

-Hey, pal, I see you over there. Don't play games with me, 'cause I ain't in the mood.

Instead of running away, he came toward me. It was that same man who frightened Jaime and accosted me in the subway tunnel. What the fuck did he want?

-Good evening.

-How come you've been dogging me, again?

-To warn you, that is, if it's not already too late. That young woman and her group are dangerous. They will ask you to do unholy things and place your mortal life in danger.

-I don't know what to say to that. Why the hell is this happening to me? I feel like I'm being shoved in four different directions.

-You've been targeted. Goodbye, Angel.

# Chapter Three
# December 15, 1947

I WAS sitting in bed on top of the sheets and still not feeling tired. On the night table was a savings pass book and in it was my name.  I had $25,000 to my name. A pay-off. A fucking pay-off for what had been done to me against my will. Enough money for a couple of years, but for eternity? Aswan had to be kidding. I'd keep in touch, all right, for a lot more money. That funeral parlor director needed some shaking down.

And, it was just about then that the horrible night began. Aswan was right: flashes of memory kept coming back to me every time I began to doze off. Every time I closed my eyes, I'd feel myself drifting off into a deep sleep, but seeing everything around me. My dreams were kind of like a jigsaw puzzle trying to put itself together: the pieces didn't fit so the unfinished picture was a bizarre mess of nothing.

I saw myself looking up from the metal table like I was almost out of my body. My legs were being held up and gauze bandages were being wrapped around them. The bandages must have been treated with some kind of chemical because they burned into my flesh. The odor was of death: it filled the room with the stink of rotted fruit. It made me want to vomit.

I woke up with a start and, then, collapsed back on to my bed and drifted off again...but the memories continued.

Now, they were lifting me up by the buttocks and wrapping the rest of me in bandages. Aswan was fondling my rod with this big smile on his face. Now, my torso was being wrapped up...even my manhood. I tried to scream but no sound came out. My eyes must have shown my horror because Aswan stroked my forehead and whispered some strange sound in my ear. His breath smelled like...blood. I blacked out.

# Chapter Four
## December 17, 1947

I WOKE up and ran my hand through my short hair. I just might have cried; but, I wasn't that kind of a guy.

I kicked the sheets off and looked out the window. It was dark outside; but I got up and got ready to go to the gym. My body felt full of life and energy and I didn't want to waste any of this. When I got to the gym, Jaime wasn't there and I was grateful. I wouldn't have been good company.

In the free weight section, I paced myself to work both my upper and lower body which I've been taught not to do. But, I had the strength and endurance to give to it. And, when I finished, I stayed on and did my usual janitor work for some extra pocket money. I didn't want to touch the money in the passbook; at least, not yet. Scrubbing floors and scouring toilets passed the time until evening came around. I wondered if Aswan would approve of my janitor's work.

It wasn't until the sun reappeared in the sky that I chose my first victim: a stranger...a blonde businessman who owned a book shop. I ran into him near Grand Central Station when the sun came back in the sky. He tried to act uninterested; but, I saw that he was queer. When we got to his book shop, I killed him and thought nothing of it.

That evening, I had me a call to make. I felt up to it because I had initiated myself as a killer. They say that the first one's the hardest. Maybe.

When I reached the corner of Stanhope Street, I made a sharp left hand turn and stopped short in front of Valerie's apartment building. She buzzed me in. I climbed up the stoop and rang her doorbell. She buzzed me in.

-Hello, Angel. I've been expecting you.

I stayed where I was in the dim and grimy hallway.

-Then, you know that I've come here to kill you.

-I didn't know for sure; but, I guessed as much. And, not that anybody cares, but my father is back in the hospital.

-Do you care?

-No. He's an ingrate; and, I despise ingrates. Get out of the hallway, Angel.

This wasn't the reaction I was counting on, but this girl was no ordinary girl either. I walked in and she closed and bolted the door behind me.

-Can I talk you out of killing me?

-No.

-But, I'm not so willing to die. Sit down on the couch. The night's young and we have to find you a more suitable victim.

-I won't-

-I won't die. You're right about that. And, Angel baby, you may be immortal, but you're not invulnerable. Do you understand that? I mean *really* understand it? You can be killed like anyone else.

Valerie sat down on the sofa next to me, completely at ease. I'd been outwitted...too bad for me.

-And, besides, I won't be any use to you dead; but, alive, I can be your best friend. Turhan gave you a lot of money.

She looked me square in the eye when she said that.

-Don't lie about it. I was the one who delivered it to your folks. He told me not to look in the pass book; but, of course, I did. Do you even know what to do with that kind of money? Probably not because you've never had any real money to play with.

-Haven't thought about it.

-By the way, have you started killing? You have, I'll bet.

-This morning.

-To celebrate the sun's coming back? How appropriate and what a sense of timing. Obviously, you weren't caught.

-No one saw me. It was easy. It didn't bother me at all.

-A natural born killer? We were right about you. And, no conscience? That's the icing on the cake. Would you like a second victim, my love?

-Why?

-You should learn to kill at night, Angel. The daytime is too dangerous: even if you get away with it, you still have a body to dispose of and witnesses might see you leave the scene of your crime. Listen, my car is parked outside. I know of this dive that only men go to. You do understand that, don't you?

-Queers?

-Yes. Oh, God, you'll have no trouble at all. It's in lower Manhattan. The kill will probably take about five minutes. You just lure him into the "john" and kiss the poor bastard. Let's go, my love.

***

Valerie's car was a broken down old Ford, but she got decent mileage out of it. And, in a little under twenty minutes, we were at a place called "Pretty Boy's". She parked the car across the street from the entrance.

-Just saunter in and look around. Let them know that you're not too easy, but that you're cruising. Lean against the wall by the phone because it's near the "john."

-You been inside?

-Yes. And, remember to take the body with you.

-With me?

-Yes. You're leaving via the bathroom window. Just shove your victim through it. Be fast and don't be sloppy.

I crossed the street and headed into the bar; there were a few young men hanging around outside. I walked in and found myself in a dark room with men leaning against the bar and a few sitting in couples around some of the tables. They all tried not to stare at me as I walked in. I saw the  wall telephone and headed for it. Just how long would I have to lean against it?

I folded my arms across my chest and waited. Time, even to an immortal, could be an eternity.

My victim came toward me. It's best if a blood victim is nameless and willing. He brushed by me. The bait had been taken. He headed into the men's room just like Valerie said he would. I followed him inside and bolted the door.

-Did you have to lock it, handsome? Someone might want to come in.

-Yes. You come here a lot?

-I'm kind of a regular. Never seen you here before. Where you been hiding yourself?

-Never been here before. A friend of mine told me about it. Said I might pick up a stud.

I could see that just behind the stall, there was a half open window: it was filthy, but it could be moved up and down.

Leaning my weight against the bolted door, my prey came to me with this Cheshire smile on his face. His hands were ready to touch and for a couple of seconds I'd let him fondle me.

-You should come here more often. Unzip your jacket like a good boy.

I took hold of him and bent forward to kiss him and slide my tongue into his mouth and take his breath away.  As I held him, I slid my hand into my pants pocket and gripped the gold dagger. I took it out, raised it and plunged it into the man's solar plexus. His tongue convulsed and his arms tightened around my waist. And, then, I could taste the blood in his mouth. I drank it until I almost choked on it and, then, I  drank some more of it.

My victim was paralyzed and had gone into shock. His arms dropped from my waist and hung limp by his sides. I heard myself making these low growling noises like some kind of animal.

I pulled my mouth away from his. What I was holding on to was a shrunken corpse; like the kind you see in some Hollywood jungle movie. His bones were starting to crumble. Christ! I had expected that; but I guess it's just something that I'll never get used to. The inside of his body felt like jelly. It was pretty horrible even to me.

I dragged him over to the stall to get at the window. By the time I got there, I was dragging a sack of flesh. I hoisted the body up and through the window. I let it fall to the ground below in the alleyway.

I ran back to the door and unbolted it, checked my pocket for my dagger and went back to the opened window. In one quick motion, I pulled myself through and dropped to the ground. I picked up the dead man and tossed it into the garbage can, covering it with some newspaper. In the morning, it would be on its way to the city dump. But, as it happened, it turned out I was wrong about that.

I walked out of the alleyway and across the street to Valerie's parked car.

-How'd it go?

-Perfect.

-Get in, Angel. We shouldn't hang around here any longer than we have to.

-When do they pick up the garbage around here?

-In a couple of hours, I think. Is there any chance of them finding it?

-You never know. There's not much left to recognize.

-Oh, God!

-What's your problem?

-He was a human being.

-Not anymore.

-Don't say it like that, Angel, please.

-Like what?

-Like...

-Like a cold-blooded fiend? A murderer? That's what I am, baby. It's what you helped make me.

-I did, didn't I?

-Drive me home, will you?

-Cigarette?

-I should start buying these. I'm getting to like the taste of tobacco.

-You really have changed. Your tone is so different and even the way you look and hold yourself.

-I guess.

-I wish I had one of Turhan's cigarettes. I'm sure they're laced with narcotics.

-I'll ask him for some.

-Angel, do you accept us?

-Maybe.

I looked at Valerie and knew I hated her. What I did that night was gonna' stay with me. I killed another human being...could I live with myself? To this day, Anna, I can't answer that. It's too fucking big a question.

# Chapter Five
## December 18, 1947

I HAD an interesting conversation with my dad the next morning.

-Angel, you look like a new man. I have that pass book whenever you want it. Your new girlfriend dropped it off. You have seen it?

-Sure. I don't need it just yet.

-You join some kind of club?

-You might call it that.

-What else could I call it?

-I had to join.

-Who forced you to?

-I was shanghaied.

-Come, again?

-It was pushed on me.  Now, I only have two choices.

-What are they?

-Life or death.

-That's no choice for a young man to make, Angel.

-When it's all you've got, it is.

-What about Consuelo?

-I always thought I liked her a lot more than she liked me.

-I think you're wrong about that.

-She's older than me and we've never even had a cup of coffee alone together.

-Maybe, she's waiting for you to mature a little more.

-It's too late.

-It's never too late, Angel. Nothing in life is permanent. Remember what I'm telling you. Everything that we have is on loan from God.

***

I never forgot what my dad told me that day. But, I had a surprise waiting for me on the staircase going out. I felt a hand clap me on the shoulder. It was that same man.

-I've been waiting for you, Angel Correa.

-You just scared the living shit out of me. You lucky I don't bust you one.

-So, against my warnings, you've joined Aswan's group of cut throats.

-What do you want from me? And, I thought you already knew that.

-I did know it, immortal...or should I say "murderer?"

-Careful what you call me.

-You have murdered, haven't you? I can see it in your eyes.

-What's it to you?

-And, disposed of your prey like so much trash?

-What of it?

-Why did you go there? You were warned, you fool.

-I did go. But, I didn't have any choice. Somebody belted me from behind. I passed out and woke up...like this.

-Liar!

-I didn't have any choice! And, fuck you! Don't call me a liar.

-Did Aswan tell you what he wants you for?

-No...not really. He kind of dodges that.

-Same old Aswan. He's a pig and a supreme egotist.

-So, tell me, what does he want?

-Immortality without the need of the kill. Not that he has any scruples about killing: it's second nature to the bastard. But, there is always the danger of getting caught and his blood supply being cut off. No...he wouldn't want that...he wouldn't last too long. He also wants blood buddies. Henry Vandor had the right idea in trying to kill himself. Don't discard suicide as a possible means of escape.

He looked over my shoulder.

-I must leave. You're now on your own. I won't bother you, again.

\*\*\*

Another hard work out at the gym and another surprise waiting for me when I finished up.

-Angel?

-What?

-You don't remember me?

-Consuelo, what brings you here?

-May I walk with you to the subway station? Or, maybe, you don't want my company.

-I don't know what to tell you.

-Are you and Jaime not speaking to each other? Have you had a falling out? He didn't work out with you today, did he?

-I guess not. We've sort of been missing each other the past couple of days.

-I think there's more to it than that. Why don't you walk me home? Jaime's not there and we can talk. I'll even fix you a "Johnny Cake."

-You don't have to do that.

-I want to. Angel, your soul is burdened with something. I want you to tell me what it is.

-I can't. And, you're better off not knowing.

-Tell me.

-No. It'd be too much for anyone to take.

-It would be a trust between two good friends.

-Let's walk.

Within the half hour, we were drinking lemonade at her house. I didn't feel like going straight home.

-Consuelo, only you could make a lemonade into an event.

-Now, you're more like the old Angel I know, but still handsome and bronzed.

-How about the new Angel? How does he measure up? Not so hot?

-He's "hot" but in a way that I don't understand. Tell me about him.

-Well, he's more defined and hard.

-Tell me what I can't see.

-He's older and maybe not so nice. Maybe, he was never nice.

-A man shouldn't be too nice. He should be decent and honest. Angel, what would you think of me if I told you that I invited you here for a very selfish reason? Jaime won't be back until much later in the evening.

-That's good.

I got up and took her by the arms and brought her closer to me. I kissed her real hard on the mouth.

-That lipstick tastes pretty good. I wondered about that.

-It looks very pretty on you.

-Let's go into your room.

I caught her by surprise when I swept her off her feet and carried her into the bedroom. I put her on the bed and undressed her.

-Slide under the sheet.

She did as she was told. I took off my clothes and tossed them on to the floor. I got into bed and laid right on top of her, balancing my weight so as not to hurt her too much...not just yet, anyway. I was already hard and I could have penetrated her and come in minutes. I held back.

-I like this new Angel. Gentle and hard. You've become a man.

She stroked my back and butt.

-Here. Reach for this.

She took my rod in her hand and massaged it.

-Careful. I don't want to come just yet.

-Now, press hard into me. You may be rough and even brutal. If there's pain afterwards, all the better.

I grabbed her hard by the thighs and pushed her against me. I rammed my rod into her moist pussy...in and out...in and out. I buried my mouth in her neck and, then, my tongue found her mouth again. My thrusting got faster and faster. I couldn't hold back. I shot my load into that moist opening.

At last, I let go and fell on top of her.

-Angel, would you allow me to breathe, please? No. I don't want you to get off me, not yet. You're still hard and I don't want you to pull out. Kiss me, again.

-I'm starting to lose my erection. I've gotta' pull out.

-If you must.

I turned on my side and leaned on my elbow.

-I can fix you another "Johnny Cake."

-You mean that biscuit and cheese sandwich? I could go for another one.

Left alone in bed, I began to think about what I'd just done. Was there a point to it...of being intimate with a girl who I'd probably never see again? Maybe it was something for Consuelo to hold on to when I was gone? Maybe this was an enticement for me to stay with her and to even marry her...maybe.

I kept wrapping the sheets around my legs, exposing my manhood that was still semi-erect. I pulled the sheets above my waist to cover myself. This was no good because it complicated matters. I heaved a huge sigh, got up and put on my jockey shorts. I walked over to the window and looked out into the back alley.

-Angel, come and sit down on the bed and have something to eat.

-I have to leave soon.

-Just like a man: eats and runs.

Consuelo had her arm through mine.

-I'll make you another cake to take with you.

-You don't have to do that.

-Will I see you again?

-I guess so.

-That's not the romantic answer that I wanted to hear.

-I'm not a romantic guy. You know that.

-But, you are. You just don't know it yet.

-Consuelo?

-Do I want to hear this?

-What happened a few minutes ago...it made a man out of me.

-You did that. And, now that you're a man, what plans do you have.

-None.

-I don't believe that.

She moved a little away from me.

-Angel, I have this terrible feeling about you.

-I have to go.

-No. Don't go yet. Please.

I got up and went to pick up my clothes from the floor.

-What have I done to upset you? I know. I ask too many questions.

-It's not that. It's just that I can't answer any.

I pulled my pants on, bent over and scooped up my T-shirt.

-Angel, what is wrong? Please, tell me.

I tucked my T-shirt into my pants. At that moment, I felt like the biggest ingrate in the whole fucking world.

-My not telling you anything is the best thing I can do for you.

-I hate the sound of that because it rings very false.

-I'm ready to go.

-Wait. I'll fix you something to take with you.

Once again, she left me alone. I put my socks and shoes back on and walked into the hallway. Leaning against the wall, I waited for her to come back. She came back with a small cake wrapped in wax paper.

-Don't forget your gym bag. You can eat this on your way to the subway; it's still fresh and warm.

I stood there awkwardly shifting my weight from side to side.

-Nervous, Angel? You may kiss me goodbye.

I kissed her and, then, turned around and left. When I got out on to the street, I peeled open the wax paper and started eating the cake.

# Chapter Six
# January 8, 1948

-WHAT'S SO bad about being sentimental?

   -It'll kill you and destroy everything else that's gone before.

   We were driving in Aswan's car on our way to some homosexual bathhouse. We needed a victim that evening. A couple of weeks had passed since I'd seen or heard from Jaime or Consuelo. I could understand about Consuelo. As a woman, she was probably waiting to hear from me.

   But, what about Jaime? Not hearing from him really bothered me. I hadn't seen him at the gym for the past couple of days. I was a kinda' worried and annoyed. Was he avoiding me? Maybe. Maybe because of what happened in the steam room or his embarrassment at the photo shoot? For now, I had to put it out of my mind.

Aswan kept talking, keeping his eyes on the road ahead.

-You think me hard, don't you? We are not like others, you and I. Therefore, the rules of the game are quite different for us.

-I didn't think that the rules applied to us at all.

-Only to a limited extent. One must lead an ordered life and some of those rules help to structure it. The kill should ideally be executed on the night of the new moon. Try and remember that. Granted, it's not always possible. I'm overdue, myself.

We reached our destination.

-I'll park the car here. We have only the one block to walk. You didn't bring your gym bag with you?

-No.

-You did bring your dagger?

-You bet.

We walked up to the converted brownstone and signed in under assumed names. We were given a towel each and a key to a small barracks type room. Aswan knew the way. The room consisted of a bunk, a small locker and a red light fixture.

-You see why I come here? Privacy and anonymity. You just lead your victim here and...nothing to it.

-You're right. It's too easy. And, no one ever misses these guys?

-They're mostly runaways and boys of the street with no families. They don't tell people where they come from. And, why should that concern me? Now, start getting undressed. We've got work to do.

We got undressed and in a couple of minutes, I was wrapping a towel around my waist.

-You are a beauty, Angel. Take off your glasses. Perfection. We'll have a boy in here within minutes. Don't be nervous.

We left the room and Turhan locked up. A few boys were gathered down the hallway. When they caught sight of me and Aswan, they openly stared. My fellow murderer whispered in my ear.

-Walk by and glance at them. One of them will follow you back to the room. Trust me.

I did as I was told. One of the boys followed me back to the room. Aswan had to ease past us to join me.

-Good work. You brought back quite a beauty. Maybe, the young man will let us share him.

The young boy didn't answer. He just smiled and took his towel off.

The three of us went in.

Our work in that room was easy. The boy was willing and eager for my kiss. The dagger went into him unnoticed. His blood was drained and his innards started to crumble.

-Angel, go back to that bathroom down the hall which should be cleared of boys by now. We need to dump what's left of this young man out the window to accompany us to your gymnasium. Doesn't matter how he falls on to the sidewalk below. Let me take a look outside first to see if the coast is clear.

It took him only a second.

-All clear. Let's go. Hurry! You never know who might come along. Take him. This is the most dangerous part. We've no time to lose.

I got my victim off the floor and flung it over my shoulder. It was already starting to stink. My towel came undone, but who gave a crap? Turhan followed me out into the hallway, closing the door. We hurried to the bathroom and locked ourselves in. If anyone came along, they'd think that we were making out.

I flung open the window and pushed my victim out on to the sidewalk below. Aswan kept his eye on the locked door just in case someone made a fuss about getting in.

-Good work. Now, let's get dressed and get out of here. Be quick, but not distracted. To all appearances, we are two lovers who have had a fast fling and are now leaving quite satisfied.

When we got back to the room...

-But, what about those other boys who saw that boy come in here with us?

-They won't get involved. And, chances are that they didn't even know the poor bastard. And, what did they actually see? They saw him follow you, but not actually enter the room. It was too dark for that. Do you see the fine difference? Here are your socks.

-I'm glad you're on my side.

-A compliment? Good. Don't forget your towel. We've got to bring them back to the sign-in desk.

And, in a couple of minutes, we were back in Aswan's car with a rotting corpse in the trunk. There was practically no traffic, so we reached the gymnasium in like ten minutes.

-Now, we do some pretty risky stuff. I'll have to break into the gymnasium. Yes. I know how to do these kinds of things and you better learn them, too. I'll let you know when I'm ready for you.

Aswan got out of the car and walked to the front door of the gymnasium. I saw him take something out of his right pocket and shove it into the lock. Whatever it was, it worked. He went inside and signaled me to follow.

I got the corpse out of the trunk, flung it over my shoulder and ran to the gym's entrance with it, not bothering to look out for any passersby. I made it to the gym without being spotted.

-Good boy. I have the liquid fluid and matches in my pocket. You ready to die?

-As long as it's someone else.

We went up to the second floor and into the free-weight training area. I put the body on to the hard rubber mat and Aswan doused it with the lighter fluid. He poured it all over the floor.

-I'll toss the match from the stairwell.

He lit one match and tossed it right on the corpse. It went up like a bonfire and the flames spread pretty quick. Aswan didn't have to toss a second match from the stairwell after all. The entire floor was an inferno and the heat was unbearable. We ran down the stairs and out into the street.

-Get in the car and we'll watch the conflagration from a safe distance. Look, Angel! Already the flames are shooting out from the windows. How quickly the glass breaks.

-It's an old building. I don't even think they've got a sprinkler system.

He backed the car down the street and we waited for the fire engines to come.

# Part Three
# The Manhunt

# Chapter One
# January 7, 1948

JAIME MORILLO had gone to Sullivan's gymnasium the day before the fire; but, he timed his training session so as not to coincide with Angel's whose schedule he knew better than his own. He was avoiding his best friend. Jaime had openly revealed himself to be a homosexual and he felt disgraced. He needed time to gather his courage in order to face Angel again.

Jaime was in the shower room and lathering up. He wasn't aware that anyone had come down the stairs until the shower next to his splashed water on him.

-Forgive me. It's my first time here.

-I'm already wet. Don't worry about it.

-Are you a professional bodybuilder? But, the answer is obvious.

-Try to be. You just join up?

-Yes. And, I must admit to feeling a bit intimidated.

-Don't be. You're not in bad shape.

-Thank you.

-I'm Jaime. If you see me upstairs working out, don't be shy about asking me to spot you. I'd like to be a personal trainer one day.

-I'll remember that, Jaime. Are you almost done here?

-Just about. Gotta' dry off.

-Good. I'll join you in the locker room. Wait for me, if you would. I won't be long.

***

Jaime found himself walking with this stranger toward his own apartment. The intentions of both men were unspoken, but understood. Would Consuelo be home? If she was, Jaime's new acquaintance's visit would be a short one.

Consuelo had stepped out to do some grocery shopping. She'd left shortly after Angel had gone.

-You live alone, Jaime? No. I sense a woman's touch here.

-I live with my sister.

-Of course. And, where do you sleep, my friend?

-I'll show you.

Jaime started walking toward his bedroom. He had his back to Aswan as the undertaker clubbed him hard on the back of the head. The bodybuilder staggered to the floor, struggling not to black out. Aswan struck him another blow even harder than the first, knocking him unconscious.

Aswan stripped down and, then, took off all of Jaime's clothes. He dragged  the bodybuilder into the bathroom and placed him in the bathtub. And, then, with his dagger he cut the young's boy's heart out with the precision of a surgeon and threw it into the toilet. However, the blade going into the flesh must have stirred the young man into semi-consciousness. His eyes opened and he screamed...too late. His murderer had almost completed the fatal incision and was about to remove his heart. Jaime screamed again, but this time it was a guttural and choked sound that came out as Aswan ripped the heart from his victim's chest.

Aswan cleaned himself at the sink and, then, gathered up his clothes and left. He let himself out and almost got to the front door unseen. At that moment, though, Consuelo came back. Aswan brushed past her, but the young girl got a good look at his face. She hurried upstairs, knowing that something was wrong.

A few minutes later, her next door neighbors heard screams that went on for a long time.

***

Marlena Lake and her daughter, Susan, were having dinner in their townhouse on the upper east side of Manhattan. They were not expecting any visitors, so when the knock came at the front door, both women were startled.

-Who in the world could that be? Are you expecting anyone, Susan?

-No. It couldn't be that Mr. Turhan Aswan. He did say that he might call on us one day soon; but, I'm sure he'd call first.

-You mean your funeral parlor friend?

-Hardly that. I'd better answer the door.

Susan opened the front door to a stranger: a woman, tall and thin. She was more attractive than pretty; one could almost say that she was handsome. She had dark eyes and her hair was brushed straight back to accentuate her sharp features. Her skin about the edges of her jaw line were taut as if she recently had a face-lift. Susan noticed these things.

-May I help you?

-You may. My name is Isolde Himmel, Miss Broder. We have mutual associates.

Susan took note of the woman's careful wording.

-Please, come in.

Miss Himmel was escorted into the living room. Marlena was already sitting there with a cup of coffee in hand. The two ladies introduced themselves. Susan took Miss Himmel's trench coat and noted the rather expensive looking two piece outfit the woman was wearing.

-What can we do for you, Miss Himmel?

-Miss Lake? Call me Isolde. And, I believe it is I who can help you.

-I don't see how. And, I don't usually ask for help.

-Don't you? I believe your daughter met with a Mr. Turhan Aswan recently.

Susan stepped back into the room and sat in one of the armchairs.

-How did you know that, Miss Himmel?

-My dear, Miss Broder, I know many things.

-But, how did you happen to know this particular thing?

-Mr. Aswan and myself were once close friends. We are now sworn enemies. We belonged to the same occult lodge many years ago; a lodge which I no longer associate myself with. I found its practices to be obscene and its ultimate goals downright dangerous. May I trouble you for a drink?

-What'll you have, Isolde?

-Ah, Marlena, good. We're on a first name basis. Scotch and soda, please.

Susan got up to mix the drinks. Marlena was looking over this woman and something didn't strike her as being quite right. She kept her suspicions to herself. Susan came over with the drinks.

-Isolde?

-Yes, Marlena?

-Why tell us any of this? My daughter only met Mr. Aswan the other day by chance.

-Nothing Mr. Aswan does is by chance...of that, I can assure you.

-You haven't answered my question.

Miss Himmel dipped her index finger into her drink to mix the ice. She smiled.

-It's a habit I have. Susan? What did Mr. Aswan discuss with you?

-His business and his need for money.

-Indeed? I should think that Mr. Aswan was financially well fixed.

-I really didn't know what to say to him. I got the impression that he was fishing for information. He did mention something about diminishing members.

-Ah, yes. Even though he's recently added a new member to his group: a rank amateur of a killer. He's also lost a recent member.

Marlena and Susan exchanged glances. Miss Himmel sipped her drink.

-Do you read the papers, ladies?

Susan answered and got straight to the point.

-Are you telling us that the recent serial killer is part of Mr. Aswan's group?

-You're an intelligent and perceptive young woman. Yes and no, my dear.

Marlena didn't like this game of evasion and dangling questions.

-Then, what the hell do you mean, lady?

-There are two serial killers.

Marlena was taken aback.

-Two of them roaming the city?

-Quite. And, could I have my drink freshened, please?

Susan took Miss Himmel's glass.

-And, Miss Himmel, you know who they are? You must tell us and the police, of course.

-No, Susan. Not the police...not yet.

Marlena asked a pointed question.

-Who are they?

-Ask Edward Mendez. He knows the identity of one if not his actual whereabouts.

-Edward knows this and hasn't contacted me? And, the other?

-Your daughter had lunch with him the other day: Mr. Turhan Aswan.

# Chapter Two
## January 9, 1948

-OKAY, MENDEZ, we know our killer is Angel Correa.

    -I guess.

    -Hey, pal, don't friggin' "guess" and don't pull back on me. Correa's our man, right?

    -I'd say: yes. But-

    -That I don't like.

    -He could have an accomplice-

    -Do I want to hear this?

    -There could be a second serial killer.

    -Like who?

    -This is gonna' be a guess, Lieutenant.

    -Who, damn it.

    -That undertaker.

-Turhan Aswan? He might be Correa's accomplice, but that doesn't explain those fingerprints we found. By the way, have you checked out Correa's parents.

-The other day; but, they couldn't tell me much. His father seems honest enough. I couldn't vouch for the mother.

-Do me a favor, Mendez, see them again. His mother probably knows more than she's telling.

-How do you figure that?

-With the exception of one victim, they've all been young men. Catch my drift?

-You think Correa's a homosexual?

-I'd put a bet on it. And, if he is, his old lady would know.

-Then, why the female victims? And, by the way, Correa's dad is up on his son's homosexuality.

-And, he's probably not too happy about it. And that chick in the West Village, Adele Locke, was most likely in the wrong place at the wrong time. She might have witnessed something that she shouldn't have. She was bumped off only hours after the waiter, Martin Ho, was killed.

-By the way, there were two female victims, Lieutenant. Remember? A young girl, Eva Ceres, went missing the other day. Never showed up for classes and no one's heard from her since.

Lt. Donovan sat back in his chair.

-I remember. Has she been reported missing?

-Her girlfriend, Henriette Miller, reported it yester-day.

-And, this was in broad daylight? I know. Just tell me, again.

-Sure was. He's a brazen bastard.

-I'll be damned. But, when they get brazen, they get careless, too.

Edward exhaled some cigarette smoke.

-Lieutenant?

-Mendez?

-Not to complicate matters, but...

-They're already too damned complicated.

-I said that Aswan might be a serial killer, as well; but, a couple of days ago at Hunter College, a pretty brutal murder was committed. Mind you, there was nothing mysterious about it. The victim's neck was broken and a few other miscellaneous bones. All to steal a piece of god-damned paper with some ancient writing on it.

Lt. Donovan nodded.

-We got the report this morning. I saw your name in there and this Henriette Miller's. The victim's body is in the morgue and intact like a recently dead corpse oughta' be. So, what's the connection to our serial killer?

-That piece of paper came from Valerie Vandor's old apartment.

-Christ! And, you didn't get a good look at this guy, Mendez?

-Never took his hat off. He was real careful to keep his profile hidden, too. Only a professional hit man would know how to do that.

-A professional hitman, not some monster. Give me your ordinary, every day killer any day.

The Lieutenant flicked his cigarette on to the floor.

-Are you sure about that, Lieutenant?

-Yes. The fingerprints lifted at the scene were human enough; but a match hasn't come up yet.

The Lieutenant lit a cigarette.

-So...Valerie Vandor is now a person of god-damned interest. And, we got ourselves a professional hit man who kills on the cuff.

Edward smiled wryly.

-And, two monsters who kill at random. And, according to my sister, Correa had a girlfriend. And, just guess who it is: Valerie Vandor.

-Could be a cover for his lifestyle.

-She's gone missing.

-Then, she's probably dead.

-I don't think so. I got the impression that this Valerie Vandor chick can take  care of herself.

-I'll put her on our missing persons list. Did your sister actually know Correa?

-She did. He even threatened her. It was during the sun's disappearance.

-We'll need her down here for a statement.

Sgt. Rayno came in and was about to say something, but stopped. He saw the look on the Lieutenant's face.

Lt. Donovan took a deep breath and pointed his cigarette at the memo on his desk.

-Mendez, Jaime Morillo was murdered not two days ago in his apartment. His sister found the body. The neighbors heard the boy's death screams.

Edward forgot to inhale.

-My God. And, the body…

-No decomposition. Just one helluva' brutal and bloody murder. The boy's chest was cut open and his heart ripped out and thrown into the god-damned toilet. Horrible.

Edward said nothing. He was trying to take this all in with as little emotion as possible.

-His sister saw her brother's killer. It was Aswan.

-Christ!

-Morillo and Aswan were seen leaving Sullivan's Gymnasium together. The manager, Randy Bates, said they looked "cozy." Aswan had gotten in on a "guest" pass.

Edward put his hands to his face.

-You were right, Lieutenant. These murderers get careless…real careless — but not Correa — his pervert friend, Aswan. But, why kill Morillo?

-Maybe, he knew too much. Or maybe he'd gotten too nosey about his old gym buddy.

Edward lit another cigarette and stared into space. Sgt. Rayno spoke up.

-Lieutenant, we just got an update on that fire down on Sullivan St. It's been put out and it's safe to go in there now.

-It's a little out of our district, Sergeant, but it's worth the trip.

-Oh, hi, Mendez.

-What fire you talking about, Tom? The one I heard about on the radio last night?

-That's it all right. Sullivan's gymnasium: the one that Correa goes to.

-Mendez, why don't you head on down there with Sergeant Rayno here? You won't be stepping on as many toes.

Edward put on his Fedora.

-I'm on my way.

\*\*\*

The conflagration had made the evening radio news the night before. The fire had spread to several adjoining buildings and threatened to engulf a clothing warehouse under construction. Area residents had been evacuated for their own safety, but were now returning to their homes.

On his way downtown, Edward picked up Yolanda who'd been waiting for him to drive her home.

-Sorry about the detour, baby; but, I'm unofficially working for Lt. Donovan on this one. Light a cigarette for me, will you?

-Here.

Yolanda handed the shamus his cigarette.

-How come you're chasing this fire? It sounded pretty bad, but they must have put it out by now.

-They have, but it started at Sullivan's Gymnasium.

-Oh. Isn't that where-

-You got it. That was Correa's hangout.

-And, you think he set it on fire? But, why should he set his own gymnasium on fire?

Edward shrugged.

-Revenge? Murder? That's what we've got to find out.

-But, can you even get close to the gym? Even if the fire's out, it might not be safe to go inside.

-You're probably right about that; but I'm hoping to bump into the medical officer, Tony. He's a friend of mine. He might still be on the scene in case they find other victims. And, by the way, that's Sgt. Rayno tailing us.

\*\*\*

The fire at the gymnasium was put out and the immediate area blocked off. Firefighters had gone in to check for any casualties. They found a body burnt beyond recognition: a charred skeleton that was disintegrating as they were bringing it down. It was now in the morgue, but the Medical Examiner was still at the scene and about to leave. Edward had caught up to his old friend, Tony Monteo, just in time.

-Not much chance of an identification.

-No fingerprints came off of that cadaver, Eddie. Must have been an employee or maybe some burglar who botched things up.

The two men were staring at the remains of the building that had once been a gymnasium for serious minded bodybuilders.

-What gets me- Well, I'd better not say.

-Come on, Tony. Give.

-Even this kind of inferno wouldn't have done that to the body I saw last night. You want my honest opinion, Eddie? And, you'd better not repeat it.

-I'm listening.

-This guy was dead hours...maybe even days...before this place was torched. And, it was torched, all right. They're pretty damned sure about that.

Edward's blood went cold: another serial killer victim. But, why the damned fire? Why go to all this trouble to cover it up.

Yolanda walked over to the two men.

-Hey, Tony, meet my girlfriend, Yolanda. The future national champion of figure skating.

-Pleased to meet you, Yolanda. Never met a figure skater before.

He turned back to Edward.

-You know how to pick 'em, Eddie.

Edward didn't catch the last part of Tony's compliment. He noticed a car parked a couple of blocks down. He could just make out the two men in the front seat. His P. I. radar kicked in.

-Hey, Tony, don't turn around, but there's a car parked about a block away on the opposite side of the street from where we're standing. Yolanda, baby? You're facing in that direction. Can you make out the two men inside?

-I think so. Just give me a second.

Yolanda focused her vision on the parked car. The man sitting next to the driver looked familiar. The figure skater tried to stay composed as recognition kicked in.

-Edward...that's Angel sitting next to that man. I'm certain of it. You don't forget that striking face of his.

-Okay, baby, real casual like, let's walk back to the car. Tony? Keep your eye on that car. You can turn around now. If it takes off, you holler real hard and point me in the right direction. Got it?

-You bet, pal. Better get movin' and be careful.

Edward and Yolanda walked back to the P. I.'s parked Ford. Sgt. Rayno was in his squad car watching them. And, putting on his grimmest expression, Edward nodded to the Sergeant who knew that something must be up. He waited for some kind of a signal from the P. I..

Edward and Yolanda got into the Ford.

-Now, what?

-We wait, baby, and play follow the leader. I wish I could make out who's with Correa.

-Maybe one of his gym buddies.

-Maybe. The two of them might be in this together. I don't know.

-Edward, they're pulling out.

-Here we go.

The P. I. followed the black car keeping a city block between them. Sgt. Rayno followed closer behind Edward's car.

-I hope Correa doesn't spot Rayno's squad car.

-If he does, then what?

-It'll be a race through lower Manhattan, for sure.

The three cars were playing tag: past Canal St and, then, on to Chambers St. and the Wall St. district which would be like a graveyard at this time of night.

-Edward? I think he's speeding up. I saw Correa looking back at us.

-So did I; and that wasn't a pleasant smile on the bastard's face. He knows that we're on to him.

Edward stepped on the gas pedal to keep up. The black car ran a red light and so did Edward and Rayno's squad car.

-Now, baby, it's an all out drag race. Hang on.

-Where can he go? It's only a half a mile to the Battery. He'll have to turn back.

-And, that's when we'll get him- damn it! They're turning on to the Brooklyn Bridge.

The black car had made an illegal U-turn and doubled back to the famous bridge. All three cars were now crossing the bridge that connected Manhattan to the borough of Brooklyn.

-It's a damn good thing there's practically no traffic. Uh-oh...spoke too soon. The bastard nearly side swiped that car.

-He did side swipe it. Look! It's weaving back and forth out of control.

-Christ! And, I've gotta' pass it to keep up with Correa.

Edward maneuvered around the distressed vehicle without incident. He was closing in on Correa's car when Sgt. Rayno put his squad car's siren on.

-If that doesn't rattle Correa and his friend, nothing will. We're almost across, Yolanda. Wait a second. He's getting ready to jump lanes and head back to the city.

-We're almost at the exit ramp.

Correa's car cut across two lanes of traffic, made an illegal right turn and went back on to the bridge. His two pursuers followed, but Correa's car once again side swiped a car and sent it spinning into the bridge's guard rail.

-Christ! Did you see that? That creep nearly sent that car into the river.

Yolanda turned to look back.

-I think they're okay, Edward. At least, they didn't go over.

-Amen to that.

Sgt. Rayno was still following behind Edward's Ford and practically tailgating it.

-You live dangerous, Rayno. If I've gotta' stop short, we're headed for a crack up.

All three cars had now exited the bridge and were once again in Manhattan.

-Edward, he's heading back uptown.

-What the hell else can that maniac do? It's his only way to dodge us.

Once past Chambers St., traffic started picking up, but they had Sgt. Rayno as a police escort. Traffic made way for them, but Correa's car was also taking advantage of that.

At the corner of Canal St. and Broadway, Correa's car made an abrupt stop. Its passenger got out and made a break for the crowded Chinatown district. The black car sped on uptown.

-That was Correa who got out. I'm going after him.

The P. I. double-parked his car and got out.

-Find a parking space and lock yourself in. Wait for me.

Edward didn't give his girlfriend a chance to re-spond. He took off on foot after Correa. And, as best she could, Yolanda tried following her boyfriend through the narrow and congested streets of Chinatown.

Sgt. Rayno saw what happened and went after the black car heading uptown.

Edward was now walking at a fast clip trying to avoid pedestrians but never taking his eyes off his quarry. He spotted Correa about two thirds of a city block ahead of him.

-He's not gonna' get away.

Correa didn't look back; if he did, he'd lose his stride and momentum. He had to keep moving like a statue come to life: a statue without a soul. He knew he was being tailed and he knew by whom: Mendez. And, the shamus probably had a gun on him. Correa was an immortal; but, he was not invulnerable. And, at this moment, he didn't want to die or be put in prison where they'd eventually "burn" him.

Edward was catching up to Correa. The street lamps and some of the garish neon signs of shops gave his vision crystal clarity. The hues of red, orange, and yellow were all registered in his retina as passing backdrops that fell off the blackness of the night...not distracting just interesting.

And, Correa vanished from sight. No. It couldn't be. A person just physically vanishing wasn't possible. Edward put his brain's logic on automatic. Yes. For the briefest moment, his eyes had registered a shadow veering left at the exact spot where he now stood: under the marquee of a movie theater. Correa must have gone into the movie theater. He must have just walked past the ticket booth and the ticket taker at the entrance. Edward did the same. He flashed his I.D. license to explain the trespass.

Edward found himself in a pitch black theater. The movie was flashing on the screen, but it must have been some night scene because so little light was reflected on to the inside of the movie house. The P. I.'s eyes were adjusting to the darkness. He stayed at the back in the center aisle. It wasn't a big theater; only two main sections with twenty or so rows of seats, but it was crowded with patrons.

Edward scanned the seating to his left and, then, to his right. No one was moving or even fidgeting in their seats. He had no choice. He had to walk the length of the center aisle right up to the stage. Correa would see him; but, he had to take that risk.

As unobtrusively as possible, the P. I. began his walk. He leaned toward the end of each row of seats as he passed and no one seemed to take any notice of him. Good. Nothing unusual and no sign of Correa. He noticed a back exit sign to his right: had Correa made his escape through there? Maybe. But, Edward's gut instinct told him that the murderer was still somewhere in the theater.

The P. I. reached the stage area and was about to start his walk back up the center aisle. Did he hear breathing behind the movie screen? He did. He crouched down so as not to block the patrons' view. As fast as he could, he made it to the edge of the screen, drew his gun and got behind the screen to confront Correa who was standing at the other end, ready to make a run for the exit.

The two men stared each other down.

-Mendez, what do you want from me, man?

-You can even ask that question, pal? I've gotta' take you in. Move forward real slow like and let me see your hands.

-Forget it. I'm not turning myself in to you or anybody. They'll burn me for what I've done. It wasn't my fault. I didn't chose this...that bitch, Valerie, tricked me and Aswan-

-You mean the cat you were just joy riding with? The two of you looked pretty cozy to me.

-He's no friend.

-Okay. An ally, then. You pick lousy allies.

-You don't listen too good.

-Angel, let's head uptown. There's no other way for you.

-Can't do that, man. I got scores to settle.

-Valerie?

-She's one.

-Maybe, she's even told your parents about you.

-Then, she'd have to tell them everything. I don't think that chick would do that.

Edward was moving closer to Correa with his gun still drawn.

-I gotta' let Jaime know I'm not dead.

This took the P. I. by surprise.

-Jaime Morillo?

-You know him. My workout buddy. I'd give any-thing to go back just one month in time and undo all this shit. I miss him. I miss our workouts together.

Edward took a deep breath.

-Angel? Jaime Morillo is dead and the police are pretty damned sure that your buddy, Aswan, did it.

-Don't lie to me, Mendez. He can't be dead. You're trying to trick me.

Correa started moving toward Edward. He was go-ing to kill him.

-Jaime's dead. It happened just a couple of days ago.

-Aswan did it; for once the cops are right about something. He's a jealous bastard and a pervert. He wants me for himself. Now, I got me another score to settle.

The two men were now only a few feet from each other.

-Angel, if this – whatever "this" is – was forced on you, we might get you off.

-Not after tonight. Aswan's plan to fake my own death backfired. I'm almost glad it did.

Edward knew what he meant: the body in the gym-nasium.

-I gotta' take you in, pal.

Correa smiled.

-Just try.

And, with that, Correa did the unexpected. He turned to face the back of the movie screen and with his bare hands ripped a hole right through it. Edward went to grab him and caught him by the leg. Correa kicked free, jumped through the hole in the movie screen and ran down the center aisle heading for the exit. Edward jumped through the screen and ran after him, firing a warning shot that Correa ignored.

Pandemonium now reigned in the theater. Some patrons ducked down and screamed while others were running down the center aisle trying to get out. They blocked Edward's path and he lost sight of Correa. The P. I. pushed his way through the panic stricken people, but by the time he got to the exit there was no sign of his suspect.

Edward now found himself standing in front of the theater's marquee. It was starting to  rain. He looked around and surveyed the immediate area: there was no sign of Angel Correa. The bastard had done a vanishing act.

-Damn it! I had him and the son-of-a-bitch got away.

A car's horn got the P. I.'s attention. It was Yolanda. He pulled his Fedora down to shield his face from the rain and ran over to his car and got in. Yolanda moved over to make room for him.

-He's on the loose, baby. And, if we don't find him real soon, they'll be at least two more dead people in the city morgue.

Edward was wrong. Angel Correa was ready to go on a rampage. The one person in the world he loved was dead and the murderer didn't care how many others would have to die.

# Chapter Three
# January 10, 1948

EDWARD MENDEZ was sitting in the interrogation room on the third floor of the 86th St. precinct. Two days had gone by since the fire at Sullivan's gymnasium. No other bodes had been found, but the place was gutted. Randy Bates, the manager, had already put in the insurance claim.

With Edward in the interrogation room were Lt. Donovan, Sgt. Rayno, and Mr. Turhan Aswan. The Lieutenant sat opposite the funeral parlor director and Edward and the Sergeant sat facing each other. Cigarette smoke was floating in the air like drifts of London fog. Sgt. Rayno, a non-smoker, was swatting away the smoke. An overhead light illuminated the suspect and kept the three law enforcers in shadow play.

Lt. Donovan began his interrogation.

-Mr. Aswan? That is your name: Turhan Aswan?

-It is.

-Are you an American citizen, Mr. Aswan?

-Of course. I emigrated to this country years ago.

-Good. You own a funeral parlor down in the West Village?

-I do.

-Mr. Aswan, why were you fleeing the scene of a crime last night?

-I'd no idea that it was a crime scene. How could I know such a thing, Lieutenant?

-Well, for one thing, you were seen loitering about only a couple of blocks away. We have several witnesses who can testify to that.

-That proves nothing.

-You think so, huh?

-I was sitting in my own car, minding my own business.

-Then, why, Mr. Aswan, were you fleeing the crime scene at break neck speed?

-I was curious about a building that had gone up in flames. What of it? There were other people "loitering" about, as well. A fire can be rather exciting.

-But, this one had been put out. What's so exciting about a  burnt out shell of a building?

-Many things interest me. The ruins of a building happen to be among them.

-Why did you flee the scene? And, this time, pal, try answering my question.

-I did not "flee the scene" as you put it. I drove off.

-With a Mr. Angel Correa in the front seat sitting next to you.

-Yes. I don't deny it. Why should I?

-That gymnasium that went up like a Roman candle and Mr. Correa happens to be a member there.

-Is he the only member? I doubt it.

Lt. Donovan tried bluffing the suspect.

-A witness has come forward to testify that he saw the two of you leaving the building only seconds before it went up in flames.

-Who is this witness?

-None of your damned business. After you left the crime scene last night, why didn't you stop for Sgt. Rayno here?

-He wasn't pursuing me. It was this man, this shamus. Why should I stop for him?

-You should have stopped for Sgt. Rayno. He had to chase you all the way up to Columbus Circle. Your car had to be forced on to the sidewalk endangering pedestrians.

-I panicked. I shouldn't have. But, I committed no crime. I couldn't understand why I was being chased.

-What's Angel Correa to you?

-An acquaintance.

-How long have you known him? How did you come to know him.

-His girlfriend's father was laid out at my parlor.

-And, the two of you became pals?

-If you want to put it that way, yes.

-Do you know that Correa is a suspected killer?

-What if I knew of it? And, quite frankly, I don't believe it. He's not your run-of-the-mill young man; but I can hardly see him as a killer.

Lt. Donovan put out his cigarette.

-Why were you in that gymnasium the other night? Answer that question.

-I don't have to tell you anything without an attorney present.

-Why was Correa with you?

No answer.

-Mr. Aswan, you're entitled to one phone call. You're gonna' be booked on suspicion of arson, fleeing from a crime scene, harboring and aiding a fugitive, breaking about a half dozen traffic laws and resisting arrest. Sgt. Rayno? Book the bastard.

Edward couldn't stop smiling. He put his hand up.

-Lieutenant? If I may? I might just have one more charge for you. I think you might have left one out.

-Be my guest, Mendez. I saved the best for you.

Edward lit a fresh cigarette.

-Mr. Aswan, you remember me, don't you?

-Yes.

-Good. You're a married man, aren't you?

-Yes.

-Good. Were you acquainted with Mr. Jaime Morillo?

-I don't know that name.

-You're starting to sweat. Don't you read the papers? I saw a newspaper in the reception room at your funeral parlor the other day.

-What of it?

-Jaime Morillo was murdered...butchered like some animal. His heart cut out and thrown into the fucking toilet.

-What's it to me?

-You killed him.

-That's a lie.

-No. It isn't. You were spotted leaving Morillo's apartment.

-Another lie.

-Last night, Aswan, I confronted your "acquaintance," Angel Correa in a movie theater down in Chinatown. He didn't know that his best friend had been murdered...and, he wasn't lying. And, do you know what he told me? He's coming for you. He knows *you* did it.

Turhan Aswan stopped breathing. He knew all too well the import of the P. I.'s words. He was afraid.

Edward pushed on.

-Morillo's next door neighbors heard someone cry out. It shook 'em real bad. Young Jaime was well liked. He didn't have any enemies. He was a nice boy who kept to himself. And his sister, Consuelo Morillo, gave us a description of the man she saw fleeing the apartment building and it fits you to the fucking "T." You were also seen by Randy Bates leaving the gymnasium with Jaime.

Turhan Aswan had gone quite pale.

-Now, Aswan, just how do you and Correa kill your victims? You can tell me.

No answer.

-Not telling, huh? Trade secret? You wanna' know what I think? I think that funeral parlor of yours should be searched inside and out and taken apart. It's nothing but a god-damned front for your shady operations. And, I think your wife should be brought in for questioning. We found out that your business is in her name.

-Leave Aniika out of this.

-Why the hell should we?

Edward turned to Lt. Donovan and lit another cigarette.

-Lieutenant? Why don't you book this creep for murder in the first? And, by the way, Aswan? When they burn you for murder one...I'll be eating popcorn in the next room.

\*\*\*

Nathalie Montaigne found herself moving into a furnished apartment in the Ridgewood section of Brooklyn. It was on the third floor of a walk-up apartment building that was situated across the street from a warehouse. The rent was cheap and the subway was only a few city blocks away and a local bus service was also nearby.

The neighborhood was passable and her downstairs neighbors were quite interesting: they were the people she had met on the elevated line a few weeks ago. She was taken aback by the irony of it. The woman she had spoken to at the time was the owner of the building, a Mrs. Grace Stone. She lived on the ground floor and remembered Nathalie and the incident. The sister of the woman whose husband had died only the day before of a heart attack lived below Nathalie's apartment.

-How dreadful for the poor woman.

-He worked himself to death. Died on the job making a delivery.

-People die unexpectedly of heart attacks. One is never truly prepared.

-Isn't that the truth? Remember that man falling on to the tracks?

-I've thought of it often, and not that I wanted to. How could one forget such a thing?

-Isn't that funny? So have I and I didn't even know who it was.

-Was the man never identified?

-Maybe. I don't know.

-Was anyone reported missing?

-People go missing every day in this city-

-Nathalie, please.

-Grace. Who knows what the hell happens to them? But, I guess you haven't been reading the papers. I read the Post from cover to cover. It's got the best city coverage.

For some reason, she stared over her shoulder for just a moment.

-Anyway, there was an update on that so-called "accident." I read in the papers that he was alive and his daughter had come for him to have him taken to Wyckoff hospital. The police suspected attempted murder, but neither the man nor his daughter were giving out any info. The paper didn't mention their names.

Nathalie shook her head.

-But, there was a man with him at the time of the accident, as well, no?

-My daughter, Debbie, and nephew remember seeing a man. Funny, how I don't.

-What did they say about him? I know. I'm asking a lot of questions.

-He had one of those "pencil" mustaches. My daughter said that he looked foreign...like a man from Morocco or something like that. Didn't care for his looks.

-Indeed. How intriguing. And, yet, he didn't come back into the waiting room when they brought the corpse in.

-Pretty suspicious, if you ask me.

-Mon Dieu! But, the man's injuries must have been severe even if he managed to survive. They had placed the sheet over his head.

-Right. Maybe, the cops had to get him out of there on the QT...if you get my drift. He might have been involved in some kind of gang land operation. Maybe that's why no names were printed in the paper.

Nathalie excused herself and went to place a phone call to Werner Hoffman.

# Chapter Four
## January 11, 1948 A.M.

EDWARD MENDEZ opened his office early that day. His thoughts were in a state of chaos. He had to get himself organized. He also had two visitors in addition to his new accountant/secretary, Miss Nella Mendez. Their mother, Isabelle Mendez, had rallied from her self imposed prison and had now taken a more active role in the daily household affairs. At the moment, she was at home with her daughter, Victoria. The Mendez matriarch had even ventured as far as the local drugstore to renew her friendship with its semi-retired owner and chemist; but, she would go no further than that establishment.

Dottie Mendez was just sitting down across from her brother and sitting next to her was Yolanda who was carrying her ice skates. Dottie was passing out the paper coffee containers and she had even brought a few jelly doughnuts.

Edward sat back and drank his coffee: black with sugar.

-Okay, Dottie, let's start with you. How'd your talk with the Correas go?

Dottie lit a cigarette.

-Not bad. Dad wasn't there, so it was just us two girls.

-I'm listening.

-Good. She was on to Angel maybe liking boys as well as girls, especially Jaime Morillo. She didn't like the guy 'cause he hung out at the apartment too much – made a pest of himself. But, get this: Jaime's got a sister, Consuelo, who liked Angel.

-I know all about her. Did Correa like her as much, if you get my drift.

-He did. That's what mom couldn't figure out.

Yolanda was blowing on her hot coffee.

-I've heard that some men are switch hitters. You know, they like boys and girls. Most men don't act on it, though.

Dottie nodded in agreement and helped herself to a jelly doughnut.

-Hey, these are nice and fresh.

Nella laughed.

-My sister and her sweets. You're supposed to be on a diet.

-Oh, come on, Nella. One little old jelly doughnut won't kill me.

-Just one won't – only one.

Edward grinned at his sisters' bantering. He also saw that Yolanda was anxious to leave for skating practice. Dottie was going to play bodyguard and go with her.

-Was it serious with Jaime's sister?

-Mom didn't say; but, I think she was kind of holding out hope.

-You do know – or you probably don't, come to think of it - that Consuelo saw Aswan leaving their apartment right before she discovered her dead brother's body.

-I didn't know. My God, Eddie, that must have been awful.

-We've got Aswan locked up and Lt. Donovan is all set to throw the book at him. The bastard just might get the chair.

-Good! Why did he kill the boy?

-Jealousy. Aswan's a pervert aside from being a cold-blooded murderer. Now, what about this chick, Valerie Vandor? You know, the one who's dropped off the face of the earth?

Dottie dabbed at her mouth with a paper napkin.

-Now that's kind of interesting.

Yolanda, who was now drinking her coffee, smiled.

-Don't keep us in suspense, Dot.

-Well...Miss Valerie Vandor paid a visit to the Correas a couple of days ago.

Edward tapped some cigarette ash into the glass ashtray.

-Keep talking, Dottie.

-She told them – now get this – that Angel was the serial killer and that he just might fake his own death and hightail it out of the country.

Edward gave out a long, low whistle.

-So that little bitch has been in on this from the get go. She might have had a falling out with Aswan...probably desperate for money, too. I wonder what she knows about the fire at Sullivan's gymnasium.

-Seems that all this trouble started when Angel's dad landed himself in the hospital. That's when they ran into Valerie and her half dead father and that's when Angel started to change.

Nella got up from her makeshift desk and walked over to her brother's desk. She helped herself to a jelly doughnut and ignored Dottie's dirty look.

-A woman's influence on a man, Eddie...and it's not always for the good. Where is this Valerie? Do you think she's gone underground?

Edward shrugged his broad shoulders.

-Nella, baby, that's the million dollar question. I sure hope she knows that her life's in danger. I got me a gut feeling that Correa's not gonna' let her live to a ripe old age.

-Why does he hate her so, Eddie?

-She drew him into Aswan's circle of cronies. By the way, Lt. Donovan is probably raiding that undertaker's place as we speak.

Yolanda interjected.

-But, Edward, what happened to Correa? How did he change? What did he change into? I don't understand. And, to me, that's the frightening part.

-Beats the hell out of me. He's been turned into some blood sucking parasite. He feeds off the human body for sustenance. I'll make bet that Aswan's the same kind of monster. I wonder how he's holding up in jail? Not that I give a good damn.

Dottie polished off her jelly doughnut and had her eye on another one.

-You're right, dear brother. Who cares?

Edward laughed.

-His wife might.

-Now, her I'd like to meet.

-You just might, Dottie.

-On second thought, I think I'll take back that last statement.

Yolanda asked Edward a question.

-Just one drag on your cigarette, please?

-Sure you're not braking training?

He handed over his cigarette.

-Just one drag, baby. Don't want you running out of breath on the ice.

-Thank you, my love.

She took a deep drag and handed back the cigarette.

-Hey, Dottie, getting back to the Correas: why did Valerie unload all this on them? Vengeance? Just being vindictive?

-Ah, I knew I forgot something. Correa got a cash bonus for his initiation into the world of the dead: twenty-five grand in a gold plated passbook.

-So that chick was after some of the blood money. Did she get any of it?

-Mom wouldn't say; but, I got the feeling that Miss Blackmailer scored 'cause mom, who's the greedy type herself, didn't look any too happy.

Edward put out his cigarette.

-You know, we could haul those two in as accessories-after-the-fact. Mrs. Correa probably knows more than she's letting on. And, I think Mr. Correa is the more honest of the two.

The P. I. turned his attention to his girlfriend.

-You'd better be on your way, baby. Don't want to be a bad influence on you.

-Edward, why does Correa hate you so?

-I'm the enemy. The man who's hunting him down. The man who's going to put an end to his so-called immortality. And, besides that, the bastard hates the whole friggin' world – with me first in line. Savvy?

-I guess.

-And, baby, no murderer is rational. Murder is a violent and irrational act. And, this parasite has to kill to survive.

-Couldn't we appeal to his conscience, Eddie? A part of him must still be human.

He turned to Nella who had put down her jelly doughnut.

-No, Nella. He's not human  I don't know what Aswan did to the boy, but it must have affected his reasoning as well as his body.

Dottie and Yolanda left for the ice rink. Nella went back to Edward's accounts. The P. I. dialed Lt. Donovan for a full report on what was going down at Aswan's funeral parlor.

*** 

Lt. Donovan had to pull strings and pull 'em real hard to be let in on the official search of Turhan Aswan's funeral parlor. He knew that he'd either find incriminating evidence or nothing at all. He was sure hoping for the former. He'd even broken police procedure by not allowing Aswan his duly entitled phone call. The bastard would have tipped off his wife or one of their cohorts, for sure.

But, would Correa tip them off? Lt. Donovan doubted it; not after his conversation with Mendez the other night. The P. I. had done a real good job of it. Aswan was now Correa's enemy and that suited the lieutenant just fine  because it left both men isolated from each other.

And, now for the funeral parlor.

The door was forced open and the Lieutenant and three police officers entered the dark reception area. The smell of rot and decay permeated the air.

-Keep the friggin' door open and open every damned window in this dump.

He got no argument from the three officers. Two of them took out handkerchiefs and covered their faces.

Lt. Donovan went to the first "state" room and looked in. Empty. He checked all three remaining "state" rooms and found nothing. He called out to the police officers.

-Go through Aswan's office. It's in back. Take it apart and double check on these "state" rooms. I'm heading downstairs.

Lt. Donovan climbed down the marble steps and found himself in another reception area which was larger than the one upstairs. He looked around and saw an unmarked door in the far left corner of the room. He approached it and had to kick it open. He fumbled for the light switch...and found it. He staggered back out of the room. Hanging from a rope on an overhead pipe was Aniika Aswan. How long the woman had been dead, he couldn't tell.

The Lieutenant heard a commotion upstairs.

-What's going on up there? I need someone down here. Pronto!

Someone was coming down the stairwell. Lt. Donovan smiled when he saw who it was.

-Mendez. Good. Come and have a look at the late Mrs. Aswan. I'd say it was a classic case of suicide.

Edward walked over to where the body was.

-It's suicide, all right. Someone must have gotten word to her about her husband's arrest. But, why the fatal maneuver?

-We both know the answer to that one.

Edward nodded and refrained from taking out a cigarette. It was a crime scene.

-Not enough time to cover their tracks; which means that there's plenty of incriminating evidence here.

-I'd better have one of my men call the Medical Officer down here. Look. That must be the stool she stood on to do it.

Edward shook his head.

-I'm going to have a look around. Oh! And, tell your men to take apart those coffins upstairs. I've got a feeling that our undertaker was also dealing in contraband. This set up couldn't be his only source of income.

-You bet. And, let me know what you find, Mendez.

Edward edged his way past the dangling corpse. Something was odd about the opposite wall. He ran his hand along the edges.

-Got it!

A small panel, the size of a light switch was outlined. Edward pushed it in and the wall slid open to reveal a spiral staircase. He practically ran down the metal steps to find himself in a small, dark room. He opened the one door and was confronted by a room that was so pitch black that he thought it must be a solid wall. It wasn't. After feeling the air in front of him, he made it to the other end of the room and found a door. Where was the god-damned handle? There wasn't any. Maybe, it slid open. It did.

The P. I. walked in and saw a brightly lit room which almost blinded him with its intensity. The room was empty except for a rectangular metal table in the center, but on it was a body covered in bandages.

Edward walked toward it, but just then Lt. Donovan shouted out.

-Hey, Mendez? You in there.

-I sure am. You're going to want to see this.

Lt. Donovan almost stumbled into the room.

-What the hell kind of a room was that?

-I don't know. But, look at this.

-Is he alive?

-He's breathing.

-But, what's he doing here?

Edward took off his Fedora. And, again, he had to stop himself from lighting a cigarette.

-Maybe, just maybe, mind you, Aswan is turning this man into what Correa is. It's just a pretty wild guess.

-Yeah. But, look at the face and hands. They're all scarred. How come they're not bandaged like the rest of the body?

-I noticed that, too. Maybe, it's part of the transformation process.

-This is something out of a Frankenstein movie. Can the poor bastard hear us?

-Let's ask him, Lieutenant.

-Let me try.

The Lieutenant took a deep breath.

-Can you hear me? We're here to help you.

No response.

-Can you talk? Mendez, did he just say something?

-I think he tried to. Keep talking to him.

-What's your name? Can you tell me your name.

What the two men heard next wasn't pleasant. It was the death rattle.

-He's dead now, for sure.

Edward almost laughed.

-That you can say, again, Lieutenant.

-Let's go on upstairs and wait for the Medical Examiner.

The Medical Examiner arrived and made a thorough examination of the bandaged corpse. His preliminary finding was death by dehydration and severe third degree burns with bruising over the entire body. The other body, Aniika Aswan, had died by strangulation: suicide.

Edward walked over to him.

-Hey, Tony, did she have any help? Like, maybe, someone gave her a good shove.

-Doubt it, Eddie. I've seen this type of thing too many times. This chick ducked out on her own. I better take her down.

-Nothing unusual at all? Yep. I'm fishing.

-Nope. Classic suicide. But-

-I'm listening.

-The area around the nostrils shows irritation. And, I'm not talking about the common cold. Mrs. Correa was probably a drug addict. I'll know more after the autopsy.

-Thanks, Tony.

In the meantime, the three police officers had uncovered a cache of ancient scrolls written in Sumerian cuneiform; these would be sent to Columbia University for translation if they made it there. The few documents the police had handled crumbled to dust. There were also a few clay cylinders with cuneiform script on them; these the police left alone. And found underneath one of the upstairs coffins was a metal box filled with what looked like opium.

If Nathalie Montaigne had been present, she would have been terrified. The Frenchwoman would have recognized that bandaged corpse as the man who had been carried off the station platform all those weeks ago.

# Chapter Five
## January 11, 1948 P.M.

IT WAS just past the main rush hour in New York City. It was a late Friday afternoon and the elevated trains were still crowded, but if one were fast enough, he could still grab a seat. People were generally in a good mood, with Friday night and the weekend to look forward to. This particular "M" train was headed toward Middle Village in the borough of Queens, New York.

And, in the rear car of this train was Valerie Vandor. She was one passenger who was not in a good mood. No. She was licking her wounds because having one's bluff called is never an easy defeat to swallow. This young woman had tried blackmailing Angel Correa's parents into handing over half of their son's bank account: Aswan's "gift" to Correa...you know, the young boy who he turned into a cold-blooded monster? Correa's mother had offered Valerie a paltry one thousand dollars. What fucking nerve! The old bitch wouldn't give her a cent more. Valerie had stormed out of the apartment vowing to take her revenge.

And, now what? Who could she turn to? No one. And, Valerie knew that that was the best course of action: to stay away from Aswan's group and anyone associated with it. Valerie had already "unofficially" left the group. She never liked being a member with no real status. And, she resented that no-talent wife of Aswan's. And, if the police were on to Correa, then they were sure to be on to Aswan as well and anybody who knew him.

But, what would she do for money? She only had a couple of hundred on her and how long would that last? Not long enough if she was to go underground or leave the country. Which is why she was headed for the Correa residence in Bushwick. She had to take the thousand that Mrs. Correa had offered and just maybe she could talk Mr. Correa into giving her more; that is, if it wasn't already too late. If they had taken Aswan into police custody, all his assets would probably be frozen. Shit! She should have just taken the thousand and hightailed it to Mexico.

The train crossed the Williamsburg Bridge and was making its first stop in Brooklyn at the Marcy Ave. station. More people got off the train than got on. Valerie didn't look up from the newspaper she was reading. The New York Post was her favorite because it had the best sports coverage. Valerie was a sports enthusiast. Had she looked up from her newspaper, she wouldn't have taken much notice of any of the passengers getting on.

In the rear of the car, a young, black couple were talking about their plans for the evening and didn't notice the figure of a man who jumped on to the rear bumper right outside the sliding door. No one in the car had noticed. A few passengers were holding on to the leather straps: some reading the papers like Valerie and others just staring out the window. All the seats were occupied.

The man riding outside the train car now had his hand on the door's handle and was pulling it open. The young, black couple heard the door sliding open and turned to look at the figure of Angel Correa. He hadn't closed the door. It remained wide open.

-Hey, man, are you going to close that door? You're letting all the cold air in.

Correa stared the young man straight in the eye.

-Make me.

-You looking for a fight?

-Maybe.

The young, black girl held her boyfriend in check.

-Don't let him bait you, honey. That's just what he wants.

Correa pointed a finger at the man.

-Better listen to the chick.

Correa moved further into the car. The girl edged past him and closed the door.

Correa knew that Valerie was on this train because he'd been following her. He shoved past the black man who shoved him back. His girlfriend shouted to him.

-Ricky! Just let him go. He's looking to start trouble.

-No on shoves me.

Ricky grabbed hold of Correa who swung around and belted him one in the face. Ricky fell to the floor and his girlfriend made sure that he stayed there.

-Ricky, baby, are you all right?

-Let me up, Cora.

-No.

-I said to let me up. That punk's not getting away with this.

-Let him go. Please! I think he's crazy.

Correa was shoving his way through the crowd of commuters and these New Yorkers weren't taking it too well.

-Hey, pal, just watch it.

-Some gentleman you are.

-If you're looking for a fight, let's step outside.

Just then, Ricky got away from his girlfriend and was making a run for Correa. He slapped Correa on the back of the head. Correa turned around and belted Ricky square on the forehead. The victim staggered back and collapsed on to the floor. He was dead. His girlfriend screamed and the entire car was in an uproar.

People standing near the two combatants moved away and those sitting nearby were afraid for their lives: so mechanical and without any feeling had Correa killed the young man.

Valerie looked up from her newspaper. What the hell was going on? Had a fight broken out? Too many people were in the way for her to get a good look.

Correa made his way to his intended victim. He pushed aside the few people who were standing in his way. A middle-aged woman was thrown against the car's door and fractured her arm. She screamed in pain. A young man hit the floor the "wrong" way and bruised his spine. Correa was almost on top of Valerie.

-Guess who?

Valerie felt her insides turn liquid at the sound of that voice. She didn't look up, but she did answer.

-Angel.

It was the last word she'd utter.

Correa ripped the newspaper from her hands and tossed it into the air. Valerie's fellow commuters looked on in horror. He grabbed her by both arms, yanked her to her feet and pressed his body against hers...hard.

-Give us a kiss. No? Then, I'll give you my death kiss...real slow like.

Valerie's survival instinct kicked in. She struggled to free herself, but couldn't. She kicked hard, but her feet kicked nothing but air.

Correa planted his mouth on her lips and forced them open. He took out his dagger and stabbed Valerie in the solar plexus. The blood was draining from her as her body went limp.

A young man tried to assist her. Correa dropped the dying girl to the floor and grabbed the young man by the throat and crushed it. The young man dropped lifeless to the floor. The young girl who was with him screamed and started beating Correa with her fists. Correa picked her up and threw her through an open window. She fell to her death on the street below.

The train reached its transfer point and those commuters who could, fled for their lives.

# Chapter Six
# January 12, 1948

-THREE PEOPLE dead and seven injured. That's the tally...that's the god-damned tally. The worst felony ever committed on the New York City subway system. And, by the way, we cam stop looking for Valerie Vandor. She's dead: a rotting corpse care of our homemade monster. And, the cold-blooded bastard walks off the train scaring people half out of their god-damned wits with blood coming out of his mouth and carrying some kind of blood stained weapon.

Edward and Sgt. Rayno sat there and listened. Lt. Donovan was in one of his hate-the-world moods. They didn't dare interrupt or even offer an opinion. Come to that, what could they say? There had been a massacre in broad daylight, or pretty close to it, on the BMT elevated line. The city, the Mayor and every public official were being bombarded by public outrage. No one was safe day or night or even in a crowd of people.

-Where is he? Where is the son-of-a-bitch hiding? He's gotta be getting help from someone, but who'd be crazy enough to help him?

Edward had thought about this. He had an idea of the general area where Correa might be hiding out. He took a cigarette out and lit up.

-Chinatown.

-Why would he go back there, Mendez?

-Aswan was dropping him off there and Correa knew his way around that area pretty damned good. He must've ducked into a building or alleyway when he hightailed it out of the movie house. He knew where he was going and how to get there.

Sgt. Rayno agreed.

-I think Eddie's right. And, if he is right, Chinatown's a small area...it shouldn't be too hard to flush him out.

Lt. Donovan turned on the Sergeant.

-You think so, huh? This guy is no pushover. But, you and Mendez, here, are right. We'll barricade all of fucking Chinatown and comb every square inch of it.

No one is safe with this maniac on the loose. We've got a tail on the parents and Morillo's sister, Consuelo.

Sgt. Rayno spoke up.

-We rounded up Aswan's "club" members; but, I don't know how long we can hold them.

Lt. Donovan banged his fist on his desk.

-Book 'em as accessories before-during-and-after the god-damned fact. I'll get to those perverts later.

Edward was curious.

-What about Aswan? I'd like to sit in on his interrogation.

-You will. That is, what's left of him.

-I don't get ya'. Is he in bad shape?

Lt. Donovan grinned.

-You can say that, again, Mendez. Just wait 'til you get a load of him. The medical examiner can't make heads or tails of it. As a matter of fact, I think he's probably waiting for us. You don't have a full stomach, do you?

Edward laughed.

-No. I skipped lunch much to my girlfriend's objections.

-Good. And, I see you've got a handkerchief on you. Good. Gentlemen? Let's go. This ain't gonna' be pleasant.

The interrogation room was the same one that Edward had been in just a few days ago. Edward, Sgt. Rayno, and Lt. Donovan entered the room in single file. A police officer was already there and he was wearing a surgeon's mask. He was standing opposite of what was left of Turhan Aswan. The Medical Examiner had been called away at the last minute much to the police officer's dismay. He didn't like being alone in the room with God only knew what. It wasn't something you got used to looking at.

The suspect was slumped in his chair with both hands resting on the table. His expensive suit that once flattered his body now hung on him like a shroud made of cheap cloth. His hands were dreadful to look at: old and wrinkled with dark, brown age spots. The few remaining fingernails were blackened and ready to fall off. His face was still recognizable as Turhan Aswan but not by much; even the dark eyes had dulled knowing that death was near. The skin was as dry as old parchment and sagging. The "pencil" mustache was gray and his once thick, black hair was falling out in clumps. But, worst of all was the odor of age and death coming from his body: a sweet and nauseating decay.

The three men who just entered did a double-take and got out their respective handkerchiefs. Aswan saw this and smiled, exposing his yellow and rotting teeth.

-Oh? What's the trouble gentlemen? Do I stink so much?

Edward put his Fedora on,.

-No answer, gentlemen? Too bad. You have to look at it. I have to suffer it.

Lt. Donovan began the interrogation.

-You have a right to counsel, you know.

-No point. I don't have much longer to live. By the time he gets here, I'll be dead.

-What did the medic say? Aswan, what the hell's happening to you?

-What is the expression, Lieutenant? My sins are catching up with me.

-Stop making with the riddles. Where's Correa hiding out? Tell us.

-Maybe somewhere in Chinatown…this woman he once mentioned might still be helping him. She runs some kind of merchandise store. Please…I really don't know.

-Don't lie to me.

-There's no point in lying to anyone. Talk to his parents or his girlfriend. I killed his lover, Jaime Morillo. You see? I'm confessing. I'm too tired for denials.

-We know. And, what girlfriend are you talking about?

-Consuelo Morillo. The one who saw me leave the apartment. I should have killed her, as well. Didn't have time.

-She doesn't know anything. Correa kept her in the dark about himself.

-Lucky for her. So...he did love her. I misjudged the young man.

-So, where is he? You gotta' have some idea.

-I already told you. I don't know. He's probably on the hunt...thirsting for blood and more victims. He's careless and impulsive. It was a mistake to bring him into the fold. He was too young and independent. I needed a willing slave not an individual. They're not so easy to find these days.

Lt. Donovan offered Aswan a cigarette.

-No. Don't waste your tobacco. I tried one before you came in. Tasted like poison.

-What's happening to you, Aswan?

-I am an immortal who is now a decaying and stinking corpse. Many years ago, Lieutenant, I was given the secret to eternal youth. I accepted it along with all the consequences. Yes. I am a murderer.

Aswan had a brief choking fit and continued.

-I forage among society's outcasts: the homeless, the abandoned, the unwanted and even the criminal element. I need blood and the secretions of the vital organs to sustain my youth. I tell you all this because you won't have time to put me on trial and execute me. Don't worry, if there's a hell, I'll be burning in it soon enough.

No one in the room moved a muscle. Edward kept staring at Aswan...was the man rotting as he spoke? Did he just spit another tooth out? Horrible to look at; but, he couldn't look away.

Lt. Donovan turned to Edward. The P. I. began his own interrogation.

-Aswan? Mendez here. Who gave you the secret of eternal youth? Is this guy still alive? Is he an immortal like you?

-Yes. I knew him by the name of Josef Antonio. He told me he was an ancient: one of the Roman soldiers who threw the dice for the robe of the Christ. I don't know that I believed him; but, I was willing to listen to his story.

-We're listening.

-Antonio had been given the secret to immortality by a Sumerian priest whose country had long expired. The price Antonio paid for his own youth? He torched the priest and buried the corpse. Much later on, he went back and poured sand in the makeshift tomb.

-Where is Antonio now? Is he a murderer like yourself?

-Could be anywhere; but, I suspect he's still somewhere in America or, perhaps, Mexico. Are we almost done? I'm very tired. I feel darkness closing in.

-Almost. How is it done, Aswan. How do you change someone from a human being into an immortal parasite? How?

-It's an ancient chemical process perfected by the ancestors of the Sumerians. The body is immersed in a special chemical bath and then bandaged for a time. When the bandages are removed, the transformation is almost complete. The final stage is to kill one's first victim. And, yes...a special dagger is used to plunge into the victim's solar plexus. Your men took it away from me.

-How old are you?

-I was born at the turn of the previous century, Mr. Mendez. Can't you tell?

-You're telling us that you're one hundred forty eight years old?

-One hundred and forty nine-

Aswan choked out that last word.

Lt. Donovan broke in.

-Aswan? Who was that corpse we found in the sub-basement of your funeral parlor? It was bandaged like some kind of Egyptian mummy.

-Henry Vandor. Twice before he tried killing himself. That night...that night on the train station. We kept him alive; but, he had no will to live. I'm not surprised that he's dead. More trouble than he was worth.

-Aswan? Can you hear me? What did the medics say?

-Baffled. Please...my throat is so dry...like desert sand.

He slid off his chair. All four men rushed over, forgetting about the stench that filled the room. The police officer backed away and almost threw up.

-Oh, my God!

Sgt. Rayno backed off and hit the wall.

-Sweet Jesus. Look!

Edward and Lt. Donovan stood over the heap of rotting flesh. The P. I. reached over to touch Aswan's suit jacket; but, the piece he touched came off in his hand.

The parts of Aswan's body that were visible turned black and were reduced to dust. His skull was cracking open and the brain matter spilled out on to the floor.

Lt. Donovan who was crouching next to Aswan got up.

-Get the medics in here with a body bag. They'll have to sweep what's left of Aswan into it.

Edward got up.

-Lieutenant? I think me and Sgt. Rayno here oughta' head downtown, pronto. We got ourselves another monster to catch.

\*\*\*

Anna Chan hadn't been honest with the police. She allowed them into her store and they searched it from the cellar to the roof and had come up with nothing. Why? Angel Correa had already escaped through the attic skylight and made good his getaway. And, from a safe distance, he watched two police officers and Edward Mendez enter Anna's shop.

-You're dead, Mendez. I should've killed your sister when I had the chance. I'll get to you.

The two police officers were about to leave when Edward stopped them.

-Wait a second, boys. I've got a couple of questions for Miss Chan. You look scared, lady.

-Because of you. You're trying to frighten me.

-Don't be so belligerent, Miss Chan, 'cause you're walking on pretty thin ice. You've been hiding Angel Correa, haven't you? Level with me and I might pull some strings for you. Maybe even get you a plea deal.

Anna was trying to decide. She knew that the noose was tightening around her neck.

-He's been here, hasn't he? I smell a man's cologne on you.

Anna Chan still hesitated. Should she tell everything that she knew? Could she trust this private investigator? Would Angel find out? That was her greatest fear. He'd kill her, for sure, if he found out that she'd betrayed him.

Edward saw the young woman's indecision and moved in,.

-Thinking it over, Miss Chan? We'll protect you if you cooperate. Angel Correa will be caught; make no mistake about that. Turhan Aswan is dead and so is his wife by her own hand.

-There are others.

-They've already been rounded up and they're scared senseless. They were Aswan's puppets and no real threat to anybody    They're all set to make plea bargains. Want to beat them to it? Savvy?

-Will I be prosecuted? I don't want to go to jail. I didn't know how dangerous he was until I read the papers this morning. Horrible!

-We'll do everything we can for you, if you level with us.

Anna told Edward and the two police officers everything she knew.

-Any idea where Correa might be or who he might go to for help?

Anna shook her head. Edward noted how pretty she was when she did that: the long, black silken hair and the sensual figure encased in a blue mandarin dress. She was wearing flats...too bad. She should have been wearing heels.

-Maybe, that girl-

-Not Valerie Vandor. I can guarantee you he won't be going to her. At least not in this lifetime.

-No. Not her. He hates her. The other one: Consuelo. He likes her. She lives here in the city.

-She's being guarded just in case. He won't be able to get to her.

-I can't think of anyone else. Not his parents; but, I do know who he's hunting down.

Edward smiled.

-So do I, Miss Chan. He even told my girlfriend. Me.

***

Marlena Lake had a late night visitor.

-Miss Himmel, to what do we owe this visit? You left us rather abruptly last time.

Miss Himmel smiled, but did not respond.

-My daughter and I were just about to sit down to dinner.

-You must delay your evening meal.

Susan was about to leave the room out of courtesy and to make sure that dinner wasn't burnt to a crisp.

-Miss Lake, your daughter, Susan, may stay in the room as she will no doubt be involved in what I am about to ask of you. And, I must ask a great deal of you.

-Get to the point, Miss Himmel. I don't like word play.

-Of course. Will you not offer me a drink?

-Susan, do you mind?

-Scotch and soda. Thank you.

Susan went to the sideboard to mix the drinks.

-Well, Miss Himmel?

-I need your help.

-In what way? I don't usually grant favors.

-I must impose upon your hospitality.

-And, if I refuse you that hospitality.

-I beg you not to.

Susan handed Miss Himmel her drink.

-Thank you.

-You're starting to bore me, Miss Himmel.

-Perhaps, this will get your interest.

Isolde Himmel put down her drink on the end table. She reached to the back of her neck and started undoing...a mask. Carefully, she lifted up what had been her "face" to reveal a deeply scarred face...the false hair had been a part of the mask.

Susan put her hands to her face. Marlena remained impassive. Her suspicions had just been confirmed. The ruined face of a man sat opposite her...the same man who had warned Angel Correa of the danger he was in.

-My name is Josef Antonio. It is I who gave Turhan Aswan his gift of immortality.

-The curse of immortality is more like it.

-A matter of opinion, Miss Lake. Mr. Aswan and his wife are now dead. Angel Correa is soon to join them in hell, I suspect. I am alone and tired.

Susan, who was not easily shocked, spoke up.

-You want us to hide you, don't you?

-Yes. I need sanctuary.

-And, money, Mr. Antonio?

-Quite, Miss Lake. I am desperate. I can send for my things tomorrow.

-You're assuming an awful lot.

-I can repay you, Miss Lake, with the knowledge of ancient Sumer. My presence would be an asset to your ongoing research about that ancient civilization. I am aware of your interest.

Knowledge and danger always interested Marlena. Why not help him?

-Put your mask back on, Miss Himmel. That is who you will present yourself as: Isolde Himmel.

-It's a personae that I've mastered.

-But, there will be no killings while you are under my roof. Is that clear?

-I've no need to kill. My own immortality is not dependent on the lives of others. The-

-Go on, Miss Himmel. You want to say something.

-The police have the clay cylinders and scrolls that I gave to Aswan. They won't be able to translate them. The cuneiform that they are written in is even more ancient that Sumer itself. But, Miss Lake, that is one of the secrets that I can pass on to you.

-Susan? Why don't you mix mother another drink? And, get one for yourself. Miss Himmel will now tell us her life's story.

Miss Himmel got up.

-May I use your W.C.? I'm sure my face needs some repair.

-Of course. Susan can show you the way. Then, you must come back and tell us all about yourself.

-Just follow me, Miss Himmel.

The two women left the room. Susan led the way up the stairs and beckoned to the first bathroom on the right.

-Help yourself to whatever you need-

-Isolde.

-Of course. Would you like to see your room first?

-Oh, that can wait. I'll just be a few minutes.

Miss Himmel locked the bathroom and studied her "mask" in the vanity mirror. A repair job would be needed, but make-up would conceal the defects. She reached into her pocketbook and glanced at the piece of Sumerian script that she'd holed for. Perhaps, now was the time to burn it along with the formulae it contained.

-Rest. I need to rest and gather my strength. It's been an exhausting few weeks and there are details that must be attended to. Those two young people at the train station…a boy and a young girl…she was so very pretty. They'll have to be killed, but not now. Not yet.

Susan was glad of the opportunity to have a few private words with her mother. She hurried downstairs and joined her mother in the living room.

-Mother, why have you invited a total stranger into our home? I don't trust this "Miss" Himmel who is probably a murderer several times over – and notwithstanding the fact that she is actually a man. It's all too bizarre, even for me.

-Sit down, dear. Mother has her reasons.

-What are they? She may be down any minute.

-I want to know what she knows. I've no doubt as to her extensive and, perhaps, first hand knowledge of ancient history. You know that my thirst for knowledge is insatiable.

-All too well. Do you believe she's an ancient?

-I don't know.

-Are we safe?

-We're more valuable to her alive than dead. But, here, take this. I've taught you how to use it.

Marlena took a pistol out of the drawer of one of the side tables.

-And, be sure to lock your bedroom door at night.

-Now, you're talking sense.

Susan took the gun and hid it in the pocket of her pants.

-Have you heard from our friend, Edward?

-Not since I ran into him at Mr. Aswan's funeral parlor.

-He hasn't contacted me about these rather unusual serial killings. I wonder why.

-He's probably been too busy. He must be working on other cases, too. It is his line of business. And, you could have called him with your information.

-He's keeping his distance.

Susan didn't respond to that last statement, because she had gotten the same feeling as her mother. Edward hadn't called her about her invitation to dinner. The young woman looked at her mother brooding across from her. Marlena Lake was furious with Edward Mendez.

***

Nathalie Montaigne was awakened in the early evening by a child's scream. The Frenchwoman had gone to bed early because she had nothing else to do and far too much on her mind. Should she try and find employment or rely on her benefactor, Werner Hoffman? She had even thought about returning to France. She was a decisive woman who didn't like being at loose ends.

Nathalie got out of bed and put on her robe. The child's screaming continued. She opened her apartment door and went out on to the landing. The screams were coming from the apartment downstairs. Should she go down? Why not? She was the curious type and it might even occupy her mind.

In another few seconds, she was knocking on her downstairs neighbor's door. The door was opened by the child's mother.

-My dear, is there anything wrong?

-My son just had another nightmare. I'm sorry if he woke you up.

-He is a sensitive boy.

-Too sensitive for his own good.

-Sensitivity is not a bad thing. But, these nightmares, when did they begin?

-A few weeks ago. He was with his Aunt Grace when a man threw himself on to the train tracks.

-Yes! I remember it. I was there, as well, and spoke to the aunt about it. A dreadful thing to see.

-My son insists that the man was pushed and that he didn't really die. And, now-

-Yes. Grace told me as much. But, go on, please.

-Now, he *is* dead. And, for some reason, Tommy is still afraid.

-I do not understand. The man died of his injuries? But, how would the child know this?

-He couldn't know it. And, now, he's afraid of the man who pushed the now dead man on to the tracks. My son saw him...and the man knows it. He says that the man never left the train station like the other man did.

Nathalie felt her blood go cold.

-Mon Dieu! He saw the actual perpetrator: the man who no one else saw? But, why would this murderer not leave the station? Was he hiding amongst us unseen? And, there was a third person also involved?

-My son says the man looked like a monster.

-A monster?

-I know. It frightens even me. He keeps insisting that the man then turned into something else.

-But, how does the child know this?

-When everyone went out on to the platform to meet the train, Tommy says this monster turned into a woman.

Nathalie returned to her apartment more confused and troubled than when she had left it only a few minutes ago. She went into the kitchen and took out a bottle of brandy from the kitchen cabinet and poured herself a glass. She went back into the small living room and sat down on the sofa.

-I must learn to mind my own business. What has any of this to do with me? And, quite frankly, I have enough to concern myself with.

She tasted the brandy. Not bad for a domestic brand. And, under the circumstances, it was quite satisfactory.

-This event has followed me. At the time, I found it disturbing. But, now, it actually frightens me. What does it all mean? A man attempted to kill himself. Fine. That is his business entirely. But, was it an attempted suicide or was someone out to kill him? And, was there another man involved, as well? The young boy's story is not at all clear. He probably doesn't understand all that he witnessed.

Nathalie began to feel the effects of the brandy. She began to relax.

-There was also the young teenage girl who was there: Grace's daughter, Debbie. She may have a better understanding of what transpired. I will speak to her...and Debbie's girlfriend...a little older than she and a friend of the family. I will inquire about her, as well.

Nathalie finished her brandy and went back to bed. The woman was frightened and with good cause even though her own life, for the moment, was safe.

Valerie Vandor's father had attempted to kill himself again that night back in December. Why? Turhan Aswan had turned him into an immortal: a predatory animal just like Angel Correa. Henry Vandor had regretted his decision to join Aswan's group; but, his regrets came too late as they so often do. The process of immortality was irreversible. And, even if his daughter, Valerie, could accept her father as a murderer, he, himself, could not.

Turhan Aswan had prevented Mr. Vandor from taking his own life...barely. The incoming train had badly bruised him. His face and hands had struck and shattered one of the train's windows causing severe scaring and blindness in one eye. Even his two companions had thought him dead.

The burns on his body were the result of Vandor's struggle during the transformation of his body into an immortal. He'd managed to rip off the bandages before the chemicals were absorbed fully into his body causing severe burns. The process had to be repeated...and all for nothing because Henry Vandor and never claimed a victim.

And, young Tommy was right about there being a third person present: Isolde Himmel was that person. Aswan had fled the scene when the medics arrived, but Miss Himmel had stayed behind to make certain that she could identify and hunt down any witnesses. She knew that young Tommy and Debbie had seen much more than they should have.

# Chapter Seven
# January 12, 1948

EDWARD MENDEZ was alone in his downtown office. The sun had just set and dusk now took over: the time between day and night. The P. I. turned on his desk lamp. He'd taken a break from the Correa manhunt and now sat back to eat his dinner which consisted of a pastrami on rye with mustard, of course, and a container of black coffee. He unwrapped the wax paper and took the lid off of the coffee container.

The building was emptying out with the tenants going home or out to eat. The tenth floor was empty except for Edward's office. He took a bite of his sandwich which was nice and thick and tasty. He tried the coffee, but it was a little too hot.

He turned his chair around to face the window. He could see the A.T.&T. building across the street. He could even see the Hudson River just a couple of blocks down.

Edward Mendez was waiting for Angel Correa. He knew that the murderer was hunting for him; but, when would he strike? It had to be soon because Correa couldn't risk staying in the city or even in the country for that matter.

The phone rang.

-Edward Mendez.

-Eddie? It's Dottie.

-Dottie, what can I do for you? As if I didn't already know.

-Have you found Angel yet?

-No. Did you pick up Yolanda like I asked you to?

A silence on the other end of the line.

-Dottie? What's up? Where are you?

-Eddie, I picked up Yolanda at the ice rink; but she did a Steve Brody on me.

-What? Just tell me where she is.

-She's on her way to you. We were heading for the subway when she runs across the street right into a cab. She took off before I could stop her.

Edward took a deep breath and tried talking in an even voice not to upset his sister any more than she already was.

-Dottie, where are you now?

-In the train station at 34th. I think I hear the train coming.

-Good. Get on it and go straight home. Now, tell me…how long ago did Yolanda get in that taxi?

-About ten…fifteen minutes ago. I couldn't get to a phone. They were all being used. I had to go into the subway and use a pay phone down there.

-If she hightailed it fifteen minutes ago, she oughta' be here soon. I'll keep a look out for her. Hold on a second while I open the window.

Edward pulled open the window and grabbed the phone's receiver. He sat on the window sill and kept his eyes peeled to the street below.

-Dottie, you still there?

-Right here. And, that wasn't my train; it was the other side. But, Eddie, what happened to Turhan Aswan?

The P. I. gave Dottie the low down on Mr. Aswan. She listened with a voracious eagerness.

-My God! You mean he just disintegrated? It's downright creepy. What the hell was he; some kind of walking mummy?

Edward laughed.

-You could say that. Thank your lucky stars you didn't have to see it. But, Dottie, I've been curious about something. Why didn't Correa kill you that night? Not that I'd want him to, mind you.

-Thanks! And...I don't know, Eddie. Maybe, he was just a little too close to home? Maybe, he couldn't get up the nerve? Beats the hell out of me.

Edward leaned a little further out the window.

-Just doesn't make sense; but, nothing in this case makes that much sense. Although...up until then, he hadn't killed anyone...I think. Maybe picking out his first victim wasn't so easy for the bastard. And, maybe, some humanity was still in him.

Dusk was giving way to night. A taxi cab pulled up in front of the building..

-Hey, Dottie, Yolanda just got here. That's her stepping out of the cab. I gotta' hang up now.

And, then, brother and sister both heard it.

-Eddie! Did you hear that? It was a click. Someone's listening in.

Edward heard and knew what it was.

-I heard it, all right. And, something else... Dottie, hang up the phone. I want you to call the cops. Get them down here pronto and you head on home.

Edward slammed the receiver down.

Dottie Mendez hung up the phone, but picked the receiver right back up and dialed the police. She told them where to go and why. She, then, ran down the flight of stairs to catch her train which was pulling in. She was headed downtown to her brother's office.

Edward got his revolver out of its shoulder holster. He got up and walked over to the door. He waited in the corridor for the elevator to come up. It felt like an eternity but, at last, the elevator door slid open and Yolanda walked out. Paul waved to Edward and started back down.

Edward walked over to Yolanda pointing a finger at the figure skater.

-And, what's my crazy girlfriend doing here?

-I want to be with  you, Edward. What happens to you, happens to me.

The two of them embraced and kissed, but only for a moment.

-Let's get inside my office. I'm expecting Sgt. Rayno any minute. You know you gave Dottie a real bad scare.

-I know. I'm sorry about that; but, I had to come and I knew that she'd try and stop me.

Edward sat Yolanda down at his desk and went to look out the window.

-I think I see him. Stay here and don't move. And, that's an order.

He walked out into the corridor and waited for the elevator to come   back up. And, then, the lights went out.

Yolanda called out.

-Edward, the lights just went out.

She flicked the light switch for the overhead light, but it didn't come on  The power in the building was turned off.

Edward ran back into the office and looked out the window. Night had set in. He turned back to Yolanda who was still standing by the light switch.

-Sgt. Rayno must know the power's off. He's gotta' come by way of the stairs.

-Maybe, you should go out and meet him. I'll come with you

-No. You stay here by the door.

The P. I. stepped out into the dark corridor with his gun drawn. He walked over to the stairwell; the steps curved as they descended so he couldn't see who was coming up. Were those footsteps that he heard?

Edward Mendez stood his ground and waited. The footsteps grew louder and the corridor was getting darker by the second.

-Damn it all!

He called out to his girlfriend.

-Yolanda? You okay?

-I'm okay. Is Sgt. Rayno coming up.?

-I think I hear him now.

Edward's eyes were adjusting to the darkness. But, what if it wasn't the Sergeant? Supposing it was Correa?

He waited. Should he call out? No. If it was Correa, let him have his fun. He must know that Edward could hear his footsteps. Was that a grating sound coming from behind him? He ignored it. It could've been anything. The building did have mice. Edward had joked with Dottie about borrowing Stripes for an extermination job.

The footsteps were just two landings below when a voice called out.

-Hey, Eddie Mendez? You up there? What's happened to the friggin' lights?

It was Sgt. Rayno. Edward turned to face his office door, but he wasn't quick enough. Angel Correa stood right in front of him with Yolanda in his grip.

-Angel Correa. We meet again.

-Edward Mendez.

The P. I. had his gun aimed straight at Correa's head.

-Don't move, pal. I will fire. Now, move back into my office...back yourself into it and let go of the girl.

Edward shouted down to Rayno.

-Hey, Tom, get a line over to police H.Q. You on the 9th floor?

-Yeah!

-Go into Barclay's office. He works late. Use his phone.

-Got ya'. You need any help up there?

-Just get going.

Correa hadn't moved.

-You don't listen, Correa, do you? Let the girl go.

-Edward- My God! He's hurting me! I can't breathe.

-Correa, I'm not gonna' ask again. You let her go.

-I don't take orders, if that's what you mean. Not from you. Not from anyone. You pull that trigger and I'll break this chick's neck. And, you know I'll do it.

The P. I. grinned.

-Oh, I know it all right. I could've had that cop come up here.

-So, why didn't you?

-I want you to turn yourself in.

-Forget it. They burn murderers in this state. Be kinda' a waste of my immortality.

-Aswan's dead. He rotted away.

-Good. Saves me the trouble of killing the slime. Now, brother, I can kill you. You'll get what I should've given your fat sister.

-You want me? Fair enough. But, let my girl go. Now!

-Not yet. And, by the way, I hate all you friggin' cops. And, you're number one on the list.

-Get inside the office, Angel. Now.

-Make me.

Yolanda tried stepping on Correa's foot with her heel; but, he was too quick for her. He tightened his grip.

The three people heard footsteps coming up the stairs. Correa could see in the dark. He saw Edward's gaze shift to the stairwell, a gesture that would have been imperceptible to most. He let go of Yolanda and lunged at Edward. The two men fell to the floor. The P. I.'s gun went off, firing a bullet through the frosted glass portion of the office door shattering it. Correa grabbed the gun from Edward; but, the P. I. held on to the murderer preventing him from getting off a clear shot. Yolanda was kicking at Correa who didn't react.

The two men were back on their feet. Sgt. Rayno was now at the top of the stairwell. He fired a shot at Correa and hit him in the shoulder. Correa returned the fire, but Edward had grabbed a hold of his shoulder and pinned him to the wall. Sgt. Rayno wanted to fire another shot but couldn't: the two men were turning and twisting every which way. He might hit the P. I.

-Eddie! Get clear of him! Yolanda, come over to me.

Yolanda ran over to the Sergeant. Edward did the same but not in the way that Sgt. Rayno expected. The P. I. stood between the Sergeant and Correa, who tried firing a shot...but the gun barrel was empty.

Correa looked about like a madman. He made a dash for Edward's office and ran over to the open window that he'd used to climb in.

Edward and Sgt. Rayno were after him.

-Edward, don't follow him! He's too dangerous.

-I have to, baby.

Yolanda ran into the office with the two men.

-Correa, you're finished. Give it up, man.

-Fuck you, Mendez.

Correa still had the P. I.'s gun and, again, tried firing. Nothing. He climbed out on to the building's 10th floor ledge. Even though night had settled in, there were beams of light pointing skyward and one of them "hit" Correa. Squad cars were arriving on the street below and a crowd had gathered and among them was Dottie Mendez.

-Correa, you're trapped. You can't escape. There are gonna' be cops on every floor.

-Go to hell!

Edward leaned out the window. Sgt. Rayno was right behind him.

-Correa...Angel, listen to me. The police are prepared to shoot you down if they have to. They can't take a chance on you escaping. Come back in. I won't be asking again. If I have to kill you, I will

The Immortal laughed.

-I'm already a dead man. I go to jail and I'll start stinking up the place.

On impulse, Edward climbed out on to the ledge. Sgt. Rayno and Yolanda tried to stop him.

-No, Johnny. Let me try to talk him down.

-Don't waste your breath, Eddie. He's too far gone.

-Edward, please come back in. He's trapped and he wants to die. It's better that way.

Correa edged further away and Edward followed him. The immortal thought of making a leap to the roof, but there wasn't enough room on the building's ledge. Despite the cold, sweat poured down his face. He looked at his pursuer.

-Keep back, Mendez. I got no problem about taking a ten floor dive with you, man.

Correa threw the spent gun at Edward, hitting him on the right side of the face. Edward staggered and almost lost his balance. A woman down below screamed. Edward was on one knee and Correa was edging closer to him...to kill him.

Yolanda yelled out.

-Edward, get up! Hurry!

Sgt. Rayno was now climbing out on to the ledge to help his friend.

Edward saw Correa coming and got up just in time, pressing himself against the face of the building.

-You're not gonna' make this easy, Correa, huh? I gave you every chance...a lot more than you deserve-

Before the P. I. could finish his sentence, a shot rang out from below. They'd spotted Correa moving toward Edward. Correa was hit in the knee. He collapsed to a squat and tried to hang on to the side of the building.

Edward reached out to him, but was too late. Correa lost his footing and fell to the pavement below.

Edward got back inside with Sgt. Rayno's help. Yolanda ran to get some water for Edward's wound from the bathroom. The bruise to his face hurt, but it wasn't serious. It would leave only a temporary scar.

And later at Beekman Downtown Hospital, Angel Ulysses Correa was pronounced D.O.A.

COMING SOON:

# Target: The Bogeyman

AN EDWARD MENDEZ, P. I. THRILLER
BOOK IV

# ABOUT THE AUTHOR

Gerard Denza has worked in the Publicity Dept. at Random House and Little, Brown, and Company in New York City. He's worked with such authors as Pete Hamill, Arthur C. Clarke, Willie Morris, Pat Booth and Kevin and Todd Berger.

He's the playwright and director of six Off-Off Broadway plays that include: ICARUS, MAHLER: THE MAN WHO WAS NEVER BORN, THE DYING GOD: A VAMPIRE'S TALE, SHADOWS BEHIND THE FOOTLIGHTS, and THE HOUSEDRESS. His noir play, EDMUND: THE LIKELY, has been recorded for radio broadcast. He is also the author of ICARUS: THE COLLECTED PLAYS, RAMSAY: DEALER OF DEATH, THE TIME DECEIVER: AN EDWARD MENDEZ, P. I. THRILLER, and NIGHT DRIFTER: AN EDWARD MENDEZ, P. I. THRILLER.

Mr. Denza is a graduate of Fordham University at Lincoln Center where he majored in psychology and graduated with honors: Magna Cum Laude.

He can be contacted at www.gerarddenza.com.

He lives in New York City and is hard at work on his next novel: TARGET: THE BOGEYMAN: AN EDWARD MENDEZ, P. I. THRILLER, BOOK IV.